Terrifying Medieval Tales of Blood, Lust & Sorcery

To Punish Mischeivous Children of Noble Birth

Terrifying Medieval Tales of Blood, Lust & Sorcery

To Punish Mischeivous Children of Noble Birth

by W. Michael Lyngstad

BATH & WELLS

BATH & WELLS

First (and most likely the last) paperback edition October 2025

Book design by W. Michael Lyngstad
All images used in this book are in the public domain
or have been used after obtaining the appropriate
licenses and permissions for publication.

ISBN: 978-0-578-27884-1

Printed in the USA

www.TerrifyingMedievalTales.com

For my lovely wife Karolina,
my R.E. teacher Mrs. Wright
(your words have never left me),
and in memory of my friend Rankine Roth
... And Why Not?

Contents

Introduction

After the Allies liberated France from Nazi occupation in 1945, my grandfather was stationed in the small French town of Lyons-la-Forêt. Not only did he have the good fortune to survive the war, but luck smiled on him a second time when he pulled an ornate box, miraculously still intact, from the ruins of what had once been a small antique shop. Inside the box was a book, the contents of which could be considered a third sip from fortune's fountain, albeit more for me than for him.

The book was a type of journal dating from the eighteenth century filled with hand-drawn illustrations and hastily written notes that my grandfather had almost discarded in favor of the intricately carved box he was sure would have some tangible value back home in England. When he finally returned from the war, yet another stroke of good luck occurred when the woman who would one day be my grandmother (pregnant with who would one day become my father) persuaded him to keep both box and book. Thanks to her, both remain in our family as treasured heirlooms to this very day.

Growing up and visiting my grandparents, the book fascinated me. I asked to examine it whenever I could and was willing to endure my grandmother's truly awful meatloaf, along with whatever happened in the restroom the morning after eating it, just to get a little well-deserved book time.

As for its aesthetics, think of The Grail Diary, Indiana Jones' father's journal from *Indiana Jones and the Last Crusade*. THAT was the book! Whoever its author had been was clearly fascinated by medieval tales, local legends, and lore, which he or she had traveled throughout Europe collecting and documenting in the journal's pages. Some, as the notes indicated, had been adapted from the songs of traveling bards who would spread their stories of mythical dragons and daring knights from hamlets to villages, captivating audiences of eager listeners. Others had been obtained from parish records, royal courts, and noble houses long forgotten by history. Each tale was embellished but contained a mustard seed of fascinating, sometimes bizarre truth that our author had managed to preserve for our reading pleasure. Many of the stories had been translated from their original language to something close to our own modern English, suggesting the writer had been a scholar, well-versed in a diverse range of medieval European dialects.

I often wondered if his/her intent had been to use the journal as reference material for a properly written novel or historical document … or maybe it already had been. After spending my college years diligently searching for such a masterpiece, I couldn't locate anything remotely close. It was then I had the idea to bring to life what had almost been another Nazi casualty of war were it not for my keen-eyed grandfather, for you, the reader. And so, with that said, I present unto thee …

Nah … that's all BS. Awesome, but total BS. Sorry!

Terrifying Medieval Tales of Blood, Lust & Sorcery to Punish Mischievous Children of Noble Birth is something I conceived back in 2020 when our generation's version of a medieval plague happened and I, like you, sat at home, working (kind of) and wondering what the f*k to do with myself that could be more productive than drinking wine at 11 am. Although the idea hit me then, I never actually put finger-to-keypad until 2022. I put this delay down to a) lockdown laziness, b) 11 a.m. wine-mixers via Zoom, and c) never being able to forgive HBO for *Game of Thrones* season 8, which put me right off the whole medieval thing for a while. And justifiably so … I mean, come on, the Night King dies in episode 3? And Bran, a king?
Whatev.

I write the tales you are about to read from my home in Nashville that I share with my lovely wife to whom I dedicate this book, my dog, and two cats. The idea for the book has its origins in the obsessions of my formative years. As a teen, I became a huge fan of Rod Serling's *Twilight Zone* and *Night Gallery* (re-runs, I'm not that old) and the portmanteau horror anthologies made by Hammer and Amicus studios, like *Dr. Terror's House of Horrors, Torture Garden,* and *The House that Dripped Blood.* Portmanteaus, for the uninitiated, are single films consisting of several shorter films, frequently tied together by a single theme. Each one featured that all-important twist in the tale of which Serling was the ultimate authority. I am merely a wannabe Jedi in training compared to "Yoda" Serling's mastery of the art, but watch out Rod … there's a song by The Police that talks about the servant becoming the master. I forget which one but, in my defense, it's totally forgettable. If Sting is reading this, no offense, but until you stop playing *Message in a Bottle* on your lute, we can't be friends.

As you read this, I'm working on the second installment of fourteen new, horrible tales. Know what that means? Franchise, baby! So, if you work for Netflix, Hulu, or HBO, you should TOTALLY consider pitching this book to your boss to adapt as a mini-series (think *House of the Dragon* meets *Black Mirror*). That way, we both get paid. Me, like, *really* well, but … you know … you might get a cubicle upgrade, right?

When writing this book, I tried to put myself in the mindset of rich kids living in the dark ages who had pissed off their parents and had been sent to bed without any pottage. Maybe they'd been posing the corpses of plague victims inappropriately for the amusement of their friends, or maybe they'd been caught by the wetnurse drinking wine out of father's codpiece behind the stables again … who knows? What was important to me, and to this book, wasn't the deed itself but the punishment—hence the name. As penance for their vile crimes against the Lord and Lady of the house, their wetnurse (the snitch) would have been charged with reading them a gruesome, terrifying tale to ensure their few hours of restless sleep would be peppered with horrific, trauma-inducing nightmares.

Other than administering the type of cruelty that even medieval child protective services, had there been any, would have frowned upon, these ghastly tales served a second purpose: education. Some I have cleverly interwoven with positive messaging and life lessons, the kind that would have undoubtedly received a king's blessing for his wayward offspring. Basically, do as the protagonist does, and you will die a horrible, excruciatingly painful death and be disfigured beyond all recognition, or learn from the protagonist's mistakes and grow to be a noble king or mighty warrior queen. Might be worth a shot with your own kids.

Speaking of kids, here's a good place to insert: *Beware, this book contains material that might offend.* Medieval children had it hard—even the highborn. No Instagram or Snapchat for those boys and girls … nope. They were less concerned with whether Taylor Swift's cats had their own meme accounts than they were, say, eating, or not dying horribly after getting a splinter. They needed to learn to fight with heavy, brutal weaponry to protect their families and land rather than bingeing the series finale of *Stranger Things* or doomscrolling TikTok reels. The kind of "trolls" they read about didn't have keyboards, fake bot accounts, and an attitude. They had one eye, stood eight feet tall, and ate babies. Keep this in mind as you read because, fair warning, these stories pull no punches. They are violent, gruesome, and oftentimes bawdy. Some would even say (and they will because, ya know, Facebook) "inappropriate" for our modern times. The title of this book should have been your first clue, but now, here we are. Bottom line: to create stories that would have terrified kids who lived 800 years ago, kids who, by eighteen, were already leading armies into bloody combat with their own four children, I wasn't writing with anyone's delicate feelings in mind.

In closing (because who reads introductions anyway, right?), I hope you like the stories more than my Microsoft Word grammar check did. And apologies for the first few paragraphs spinning the tale about my grandfather's WWII mystery find. I totally could have gone with that, and you would have never known the difference, but like a chivalrous knight, I went with honesty on this one. It did sound great, though, right? You had better take a screenshot of this part because I may rethink the whole honesty thing for a second press and/or Netflix deal. Also, the part about my grandmother's meatloaf is true. She's dead, so won't be offended by me telling you that. Worst case scenario, she returns as a malevolent entity to haunt me, and I write about it. So, win-win.

Lastly, and most importantly, a word to all the Medieval Accuracy/Grammar/Spelling Police in the house who are rubbing their hands together and preparing to be appalled. I do not live in the Kingdom of Mercia in the year 879. I live in Nashville, Tennessee, although our roads and some of our infrastructure are comparable. I write these macabre little tales for fun. Once completed, I read them back to my wife in a silly yet oddly period-correct pirate-type accent she seems to enjoy after an evening cocktail on the back deck. That being said, Medieval Accuracy/Grammar/Spelling Police … you are officially off duty as of now. If my "thine" should be "thy" or "ye" a "thee," or if I custom-created a few extra words that I imagine Brave Sir Robin the Not-Quite-So-Brave-As-Sir-Lancelot would say as he's running away from The Three-Headed Giant, then so be it. You try rhyming something with "wolf" or "opus," and we'll talk.

As you read the book, remember—it's FAKEspeare, not Shakespeare. Although I have endeavored to use the correct conjugation of archaic

English verbs I vaguely remember from high school, I may have fallen short. Let's just call the liberties I've taken "poetic license" and blame them on me watching *The Witch* one too many times. Some words and phrases might be technically wrong, but they sound like something Black Phillip would have whispered to Thomasin and roll off the tongue easier than a lie on a first date, so relax. Sure, Robin Hood and Anne Boleyn might be horrified, but unless they've suddenly got Prime accounts, I think we're safe.

Until we meet again in Volume 2 … Anon!

PS: If your book club decides to take a break from whatever Oprah is hocking this week and reads this book instead, I'd be honored to join your peeps on a Zoom call to discuss. That way, you can't throw tomatoes, and I don't have to spring for a plane ticket. Plus, as a special bonus, I'll throw in an unpublished chapter exclusively for you. The offer's good, at least until that Netflix deal happens.
Email inquiries to: info@TerrifyingMedievalTales.com

A Creature of Habit
(The Curious Tale of Friar Lee)

An odd occurrence said to be true. 14th century, England.

A tale of curiosity
Like none you've heard I vow to thee,
Concerns the fate of Friar Lee
'Fore taking vows of chastity,
Whispers say, "he" once was "she."

The Friar were a portly man,
'Neath habit, they say, bound tight his glands,
But fair of face and soft of hands
Seemed nothing more than happenstance,
Though tempted, dared not take chance
To lift his robes and have a glance.

The wives that gossiped on the green
Told tales of bloody rags they'd seen
Cast down the well from whence he'd been
Each month, suggesting king were queen,
Or bit of both and in-between.

Blessed are, said he, the meek,
On Sundays from the pulpit speak
He did in Latin and in Greek
With a dulcet voice and rosy cheeks.
Decided I within a week
To hatch a plot and have a peek.

With a belly full of mead and guile
Next Sunday when he walked the aisle
With offering plate and gentle smile,
I put my plan to test and trial.

I grabbed the rope wound 'round his waist
That kept his habit closed in place,
And tugging to the floor with haste,
Revealed no woman, pure and chaste,
But something more ... with eyes ... and face.

See, the robes that Lee wore weren't to hide
He were never a groom, but really the bride.
'Twas something much darker lurking inside;
A secret uncovered, discoverers died
Lest they tell another where brother resides.

For none alive on God's green earth
Knew of the twin conjoined at birth's
Obscene and twisted smile of mirth
Amid the Friar's flab and girth.

The abomination nay seemed real,
And explained why Friar Lee concealed
His body 'neath habit, lest be it revealed;
Took holy oath, with God as shield.

'Twixt folds of flesh there rose a head,
Caused widow Carter's heart t'stop dead,
And more to faint and shriek with dread
As human form took shape and said:
"Come closer lad," and spying its prize,
It glared at me with hungry eyes,
Bit down with teeth sharp as scythes,
And taking two fingers, sealed its demise.

Both freak and Friar dragged did we
To the village square; tied both to a tree,
Then with an axe cut brother free
'Fore disemboweling both it and he.
As flames burned flesh, they screamed and moaned,
And rocks we threw cracked burning bone
Till blade and fire and hurling stone
Sent both back down to Satan's throne!

Epilogue:

Those bloody rags cast down the well
Now thinking back, had a putrid smell.
"Remains of rats," deduced the wives,
Hidden there from prying eyes,
Fed Lee to his twin to keep it alive.

"Perhaps," said one, "no, it couldn't be ...
The notion's too evil, even for Lee!
A child went missing, remember ye?
Then lost were two ... one more made three,
Till fourteen count had come to be."
Taken by wolves or boars, or bears
We thought till then, the knowing stares
As suddenly all became aware
'Twere freak that feasted on flesh and hair,
And innocent bones of the young and fair.

Thus, I promised a tale like none you've heard;
I'd say yes to an ale if I've kept my word.
I can still raise a cup 'twixt fingers three,
The ones that remain, not taken from me
By whatever it was that never should be,
Hid 'neath the robes of Friar Lee.

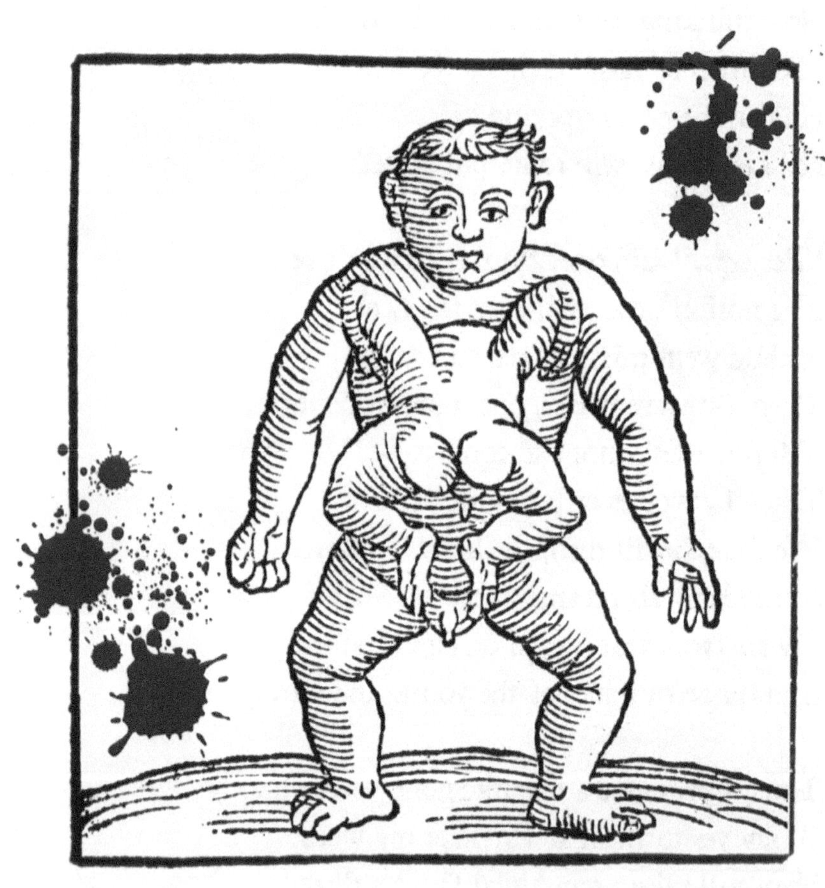

"The abomination nay seemed real and explained why Friar Lee concealed his body 'neath habit, lest be it revealed."

That Which Walks in Hailsham Woods

English folklore. Circa 15th century.

That which walks in Hailsham Woods
Is ashen bone, beneath a hood;
An evil stalks that means no good,
A voice that whispers nigh ye stood.
Pray, stay ye clear, as well ye should,
When twilight falls 'pon Hailsham Woods.

That autumn day I ventured there
To Hailsham's bustling market square,
Bartering to sell my wares
Of rhubarb, apples, plums, and pears,
I took my leave to sip on mead,
A tired trader's earned reprieve,
As sunset cast its crimson hue
Across the square, as traders do,
I rested by the tavern fire
Where tongues of rogues' hushed tones conspire,
And lit my pipe to smoke and sup,
Devouring pie betwixt each puff.

'Twas near the night's impending end,
When ale turns strangers into friends,
I noticed on a wall there penned
A poem; t'ward its words did wend.
And there, by candle's dancing light,
Beheld the quill's arced, artful bight,
Then shivered at the author's plight
As read what dread compelled him write:

That which walks in Hailsham Woods
Is ashen bone, beneath a hood;
An evil stalks that means no good,
A voice that whispers nigh ye stood.
Pray, stay ye clear, as well ye should,
When twilight falls 'pon Hailsham Woods.

Then looking closer at the verse,
I spied the scribe had scribbled terse
An epilogue to end his tale,
Yet seemingly his quill had failed.
Or mayhap, someone wiped it clean,
Preventing those disposed to glean
What warning words he did impart
Upon those predisposed to start
Their venture to the woods despite
His caution, granting all respite.

Till all were gone, and none remained,
I kept my curious urge contained,
Then of the old Inn Keeper asked
What strange events had come to pass
That drove the one who wrote to write
All that I'd read upon that night.
But all the Keeper did was stare
And fix me in his fearful glare,
Then pointed to a vacant chair
Beside his wife with cautious air.

As wary eyes began to chide
Her eyebrows' leery arch belied
Desire within to speak what lore
Forewarned of what awaits in store.
Her lips sealed, secret held at bay,
Yet fear upon her face betrayed
The fate of those who dared to stray;
The foolish few who went that way.

"The poem o'er the fire there placed,"
Said she, wet brow'd and white of face,
"Serves to warn those passing through
Our market town, as many do,
Of what it is that can't be seen,
Nor chased away, nor cleansed or cleaned,
Which prowls the cursèd forest green;
The fern and thornbush, lurking 'tween.

Where it came from none here know,
But when day wanes, dusk's amber glow
Wakes beneath the soil what sleeps;
A twisted, tortured soul that shrieks.
So if ye think to walk alone,
And hear its disembodied moan,
Run, 'fore scratching bone be known,
Sharp as daggers, cold as stone.
Take heed, ye, of its icy hold,
For once it grasps, it shan't let go!"

My throat was dry and hard I swallowed,
Holding back the breaths that followed,
Shook by what it was I'd heard,
Each pause to cause effect, and word,
I supped my wine to whet my whistle,
For wine may serve as shield and missal,
And asked her what then were the lines,
Bound within the rhyme's confines,
Missing from the poem's end
The poet's artful quill had penned
Whose truth had vanished, thinned and frayed,
And what it might have once conveyed.

The woman did not know, she claimed,
And 'pon the hour placed her blame
As ushered me outside the door
To take my hurried leave before
More questions of her I could ask;
This scourge of Hailsham Woods unmask.

So sheltering inside my cart
I readied for an early start,
And lay my head upon the bed
Of hay, but as I lay, instead
Of peaceful slumber, all I saw,
Tossing on my bed of straw,
Were visions of the thing that walked
And through the woods of Hailsham stalked.

I dreamt one evening as I strolled
O'er rolling fields of Dunny Wold,
I felt the urge to look behind
From whence I came; there, undefined,
I spied what looked like tar-black gauze
On yonder hill, then taking pause,
I watched as this, caught by the wind,
Whipped around the thing within
That raised its arms of pallid bone,
Wailing baleful tortured moans,
And ran at an unnatural pace,
Revealing then its death-white face,
A skull 'neath mottled, rotting flesh;
Its jaw, an open void, as threshed
And flailed and trailed, then as I woke,
Wet with sweat and breathless, choked.

What was this horror which I saw?
This terror with its tearing claws
And visage of grotesque decay,
Disfigured as it skulked and swayed,
And ran with otherworldly speed
O'er hills, far from the ferns and trees,
Back where it haunts the woodland realm
Of silver birchwood, oak and elm,
Stalking me by twilight's gloam,
Back to Dunny Wold, my home.

Upon the morrow's dawning light,
Awakening from that restless night,
I ate an apple from my cart
And then a plum; both soft and tart.
With all my stock about to rot
I thought to toss the lot I'd got
And hurry home where came I whence,
Then hie to Hailsham's market, hence
I journeyed forth for several hours
Beleaguered by a crop that soured,
A cartwheel, cracked and weathered gray;
Despite exhausted horse's brays,
I reached my farm and loaded fruit
Upon my cart, still resolute,
I hastened back along the road
And t'ward the market briskly strode,
Till finally, Hailsham came in sight
As dusk did evanesce to night.

Before me lay the only trail,
Receding 'twixt the wooded veil
Of Hailsham Woods, at twilight's crest;
I signed the cross across my chest;
A whispered prayer, this rogue be blessed,
As slowly I approached the nest.
There, through the branches' tangled web
A pathway cut did flow and ebb;
The evening, silent, eerie, still ...
No bird call, breeze, or cricket's trill.
The sky, an autumn orange, glowed,
As sunset wove portentous ode,
A chill wind pierced my cloak; I strode,
My horse before the cart she towed.

A few steps in, she bucked and reared,
Her black eyes, pools reflecting fear.
This stubborn nag refused to lift
A hoof t'ward the tangled drift;
And as I tried to give her calm,
She neighed and grunted her alarm,
Bolting with the cart and fruit.
Alone stood I to face the brute
And seek the truth, defy the myth,
Through Hailsham Woods I ventured swift.

This fabled scourge of infamy
That rends the wood's serenity,
A sense of dread about me spread,
As shadows thickened where I'd tread.

What happened next, I'll ne'er forget,
For it has not left my nightmares yet.

I heard my name, clear, in my ear,
Called by something standing near
That pressed its lips against my hole
And shook me to my very soul.
A voice that haunts and taunts me still;
Echoes, passing time can't kill.
Words of warning, spoken shrill,
Whispered with death's languid chill:

"Ere I be, now ere with thee,"

'Twere the disembodied, grim decree
That pierced my heart and stopped my breath,
And thwarts my gentle slumber yet.

Then, as I turned, I felt its hand.
Five digits 'cross my shoulder fanned,
And scratched with blades for nails as tore
The tunic what atop I wore;
Clawing, pawing, as I ran
Through thorns and nettles' arching fan,
Until I could not tell the cause,
If brambles, thorn, or spirit's claws
Were ripping fiercely at my flesh,
As leaping through the tangled mesh,
At last I reached the forest's end,
And t'ward the tavern ran to mend!

Silent, went the drinkers' songs,
Romanticizing days long gone,
As through the tavern's door I lunged,
And t'ward the floor of straw I plunged.

Slowly, lifted to my feet
And placed upon a wooden seat,
The old Inn Kepper brought me ale
And gently bade me tell my tale
Of what I witness on that path,
And how my presence wrought the wrath
Of that which walks, yet knows not why,
Stalking twilight's passerby,
'Neath sackcloth black, its bones bone dry,
Moaning low its hollow cry.

"What did it whisper?" one did say.
"What words, precisely? Let us weigh
That which it said, for what it means;
To some it murmurs, t'others, screams.
Yet he who wrote the poem yon,
Inked with quill the brick upon,
We know not what, but some here say,
The specter followed him away,
And till he died, there at his side,
A shadow trailing yon did glide.
His every motion, every stride,
The ghost would linger, watch, and chide."

"*Ere I be, now ere with thee,*
Was what it said," I said to he,
And watched the crowd, now gathered 'round,
Vexed by how my tale unwound,
Till one spoke thusly unto me:
"*Before I was. Now before with thee,*
Makes little sense, but then these words,
Startled, might you have misheard?

For *ere I be,* means 'once I was.'
Ere with thee rings not true, because
The ghost was not with thee before.
Perhaps it said, e'er ... evermore?
For once it lived, now dead, it haunts
And those within the woods it taunts.
Thus, *Ere I be, now e'er with thee,*
Means with you, it shall always be!"

Then overhead, a thunderous peal;
As lightning struck, its flash revealed
Outside, beyond the window, stood
A figure draped in cloak and hood.
With jutting bone in argent sheen
’Neath moonlight’s luster, silver beams
Bathed the wraith of rotted death;
None dared to blink, nor draw a breath;
For that which walks yet knows not why
Made neophytes of doubting eyes
And good and Godly men forsake,
Enslaved by fear, their precious faith.

And from that fateful, dreadful night,
Ne’er did it stray far from my sight;
The figure draped in tar-back gauze
E’er trailing in the distance was.
No rhyme nor reason, quest or cause,
Governed not by mortal laws.
Where I went, so there went he,
And thus, I solved the mystery
Of what that poet, ’pon the wall,
By madness driven, might have scrawled:

For if, when walking, you might hear
A voice like ice inside your ear,
Say, "Ere I be, now e'er with thee,"
Run, but know its shape you'll see,
Awake, asleep, 'pon land, o'er sea
  ... For haunted, you will always be.

Author's Note: Hailsham is a town in East Sussex, England, mentioned in the Domesday Book as *Hamelesham*. Inhabited since the Neolithic age, it was an Ancient British settlement that existed before the Romans invaded Kent and Sussex in 43 AD. In 1252, Henry III granted the town a Market Charter, and to this day, a monthly farmers' market and weekly stall markets are held in the town center.

The route taken by the fruit trader in the story is thought to be a trail leading from Herstmonceux to Boreham Street. Today, this trail takes you along paved roads, narrow lanes, rougher farmland, and woodland paths as you wind past the nearby grounds of Herstmonceux Castle. The ancient trail is popular with hikers, runners, and walkers, but they are almost certainly tourists or individuals who are new to the area, unfamiliar with its history, superstitions, and lore.

Locals, who know better, are rarely seen to wander these paths. And never at twilight.

The Mermaid & The Fisherman

Old Wives' Tale, 15th century, Denmark.

Lonely, drunk, and solitary,
A fisherman by trade was he.
Each moonlit morning, stroke of three,
He'd sail and cast his net to sea,
Ne'er dreaming nothing more could be.

He were half a bottle down of grog
That day when spied a shape thought odd
Amongst the haddock, crab, and cod,
Dredged up by fate or grace of God,
Trapped in twine from the line of his rod.

Through drunken eyes he thought deceiving,
Pulled net to boat, still disbelieving
Davy Jones gave up his queen,
What name he forgot, from legends gleaned
Were no woman or fish, it seemed,
But half and half and in-between.

A beauty she were, wrapped in his rope,
So back to shore he sailed in hope
She'd cook and keep hushed when he'd tope,
And in his world try hard to cope;
In time would slowly come to favor
He who from net had saved her,
From wifely duties never waiver,
Loving well this lonely sailor.

But when she woke up from her haze,
Wrapped in blankets, fair her gaze,
Tuned quick to show that land men's ways
Weren't laws she'd bide to bind her days,
So scream did the Siren, t'ward the waves.

Like naught he'd heard or would again,
Her cry did rend his ears, in pain,
This din the fisherman fought to restrain
With a rag in her mouth, and a knife to her vein.

"You're mine," said he, "and here you'll be;
No longer shall ye roam the sea!
You'll keep my cup full faithfully,
And there is no begging, prayer, or plea
Can stop you now from pleasing me
In ways I'll soon discover on thee!"

So clean did the Mermaid, and cook, and fuck,
But every eve when midnight struck,
With every ounce of courage plucked,
She'd leave the house and try her luck.
What strength could muster she from inside,
On belly crawled t'ward ebbing tide,
To flee her fate as slave and bride
Of the human mate she'd long despised.

And each night 'pon the pebble shore
When strength was spent and limbs were sore,
She heard his boots come running, for
He'd never let Poseidon score
What darned his socks and swabbed the floor,
And warmed his bed like a thrup'ney whore.

And so decided he one night
To put an end to her midnight flight;
Cut fins from tail, and to the chair
Bound both her wrists with flowing hair,
Then callously positioned she
By a window looking out to sea
To stare each hour longingly
At something he forbade could be.

Now mariners of ancient times
Told tales of creatures in their rhymes.
Women fair from waist to head
And dolphin-like below, they said,
Would drag men down to the depths for fun
And watch as water filled their lungs,
So said the stories sailors spun,
Sodden drunk on grog and rum.

Thought the fisherman, "these tales deceive!"
Some legends, though, should be believed,
For in each yarn, a mustard seed
Of truth exists for all to heed.
Sat in her chair, each day as grieved,
Knew the Mermaid what she must achieve.

Though missing fins and two foot long
Of tail, the beauty still had tongue,
So when her master fell asleep,
Slumped, numb with rum, 'cross straw floor heaped,
She'd summon help from down in deep;
Revenge 'pon callous captor seek.

Crabs in hundreds fist obeyed,
Came marching to her serenade,
And slippery eels some 8ft long,
Slithered t'wards the Siren's song,
Till cottage filled with ocean's throng
Set to work to right the wrong
And take her back where she belonged.

First lobster claws plucked out his eyes,
Then eels and crabs grabbed feet and thighs,
And dragged him, 'spite the screams and cries,
T'ward the lapping waves outside.

And once more in her wet domain,
Her fins and tail grew back again.
And something more, so legends say,
Black eyes like pearls, to pallid gray
Her skin did change, hair fell away,
Grew sharp her teeth and claws to flay.

For Mermaids sailors meet at sea
Appear as men would have them be,
But back in the currents 'neath the tide,
Lure hopeless hearts to suicide;
True form they take, no more they hide,
And shed no tears for them what died.

But a drowning death is quick, pain-free,
No fitting end for one like he,
So an octopus she did command
A shiv of coral from the sand
Be placed into her vengeful hand.

And floating in the ocean black,
Below a shark moved for attack;
Bit off his legs below the knee;
The shiv made sure he'd squat to pee,
And same as he had done to she,
Changed nature of what beast he be,
Ne'er more to fish, or fuck, or see,
Or Siren slaves pluck from the sea.

"Women fair from waist to head and dolphin-like below, they said,
would drag men down to the depths for fun,
and watch as water filled their lungs."

The Black Knight's Apprentice

England 1380. Attributed to Philippa of Clarence.

Author's Note: *The Book of Punishments* is an infamous collection of eight dreadful tales written by Philippa of Clarence (née Plantagenet) for the express purpose of having them forcibly read to her naughty children at bedtime, should their behavior warrant such harsh discipline. Years ago, I managed to obtain one of the stories, *Four Rubies*, at an auction featuring items from her son, Roger Mortimer's estate. It was a huge find, given it is the only story from the collection thought to have survived the six-hundred-year span of history; the remaining seven stories are either hidden, lost, or were most likely destroyed over the years due to the Church's condemnation of their content.

That was the accepted, unchallenged narrative, until recently, when I was invited to England to examine the contents of a mysterious locked box discovered during the renovation of a stately home. The name and location of the home I will keep to myself, per the owner's request. So too the name of the owner, a duchess, who discovered the box in her attic, and whom I shall refer to simply as D.

D and I share a mutual friend who recommended that she reach out after informing her of my (albeit limited) knowledge of medieval horror and fascination with Philippa's work. Her excited email to me stated that the box she had found contained eight pages, remarkably well preserved given their ripe old age, neatly torn from a book. She had heard tell of an old family tradition whereby her ancestors used to read "a horrific story" every year on the eve of the Feast of All Saints' Day—what we now call Halloween night. To the best of D's recollection (she had heard about this tradition as a young girl), her grandfather had mentioned the story being gifted to the family by Henry "Hotspur" Percy in the latter part of the fourteenth century.

Given that Percy's wife had been Lady Elizabeth Mortimer, daughter of Philippa Plantagenet, D had concluded that there was a very real possibility the pages could belong to Philippa's original lost work. I re-read the last line of her email over and over, the knot in my gut tightening each time as the historical weight of her claim began to settle. The possibility was absurd. Impossible. And yet, I couldn't shake the feeling that something long buried was clawing its way back into the light. Could a lost piece of Philippa's condemned collection *truly* have resurfaced again after six centuries?

The timing of D's initial email was perfect. I was halfway through the book you are now reading, and the thought of discovering a lost chapter from the mother of all medieval horror collections to include in my own was irresistible. I called D at once to accept. Although delighted, something in the tone of her voice seemed odd, suggesting she might have been equally as satisfied had I declined her offer—a courtesy, I sensed, more for my sake than hers. After a few minutes of conversation, my suspicion was confirmed.

According to D, just prior to our speaking, she had finally found the time to settle down and read the story for herself. After doing so, she had become utterly convinced beyond any doubt whatsoever that the pages were Philippa's. In her own words, she had found them "unexpectedly disturbing" and "better off left in the attic to rot."

I arrived in England the week after our phone call, eager to examine the pages for myself. After reading them, I shared D's conviction regarding their authenticity, as well as her misgivings. There was no doubt in my mind that the pages originally belonged to *The Book of Punishments*. The writing style, tone, and content were unmistakably Philippa's. Even certain lines (the morbid ones, underlined in red ink) were a perfect match for what I had seen in the original manuscript of *Four Rubies*. Despite my initial exuberance, however, I later found myself doing some unexpected soul-searching about whether the story they contained truly belonged in this book.

Why, you ask?

Roger Mortimer once publicly claimed that he and his siblings had been traumatized as children by *The Book of Punishments* and by what he called "the manifestations of their mother's cruel and unholy imagination." Suffice it to say, I now have some first-hand insight into the true depths of Philippa's depraved fantasies, deft storytelling, and dark nature. You are about to gain that insight as well, because after much deliberation, and with the hesitant permission of its owner, I am presenting it to you, dear reader, and to the world, for the first time. Until now, the Duchess and I, along with a circle of her distant ancestors huddled together fireside on a chilly Halloween night all those years ago, are the only ones who know what awaits you.

Consider this a polite warning.

Should anyone out there have the remaining chapters of *The Book of Punishments* in their possession, or know where they might be, I respectfully ask that you keep that information to yourself. As the old saying goes, some things are better lost to antiquity, never to be heard from again.

The Plague and smallpox are two I can name offhand.

The Black Knight's Apprentice just might be the third.

nabelle, dear Anabelle,
God did fashion as a girl,
Dreamt of living as man,
So carefully devised a plan.
Abandoning her silken gowns,
Cut short her hair and bound her mounds.
Her heart with joyous mirth resounds
To rise a knight's apprentice crowned.

A tourney once a year was held
Where sons of nobles, so compelled
To serve as squire to a knight,
Might joust, and 'twixt them boldly fight,
Thus, Anabelle's (now Adam's) sight
Was set upon opponents' blight.
Yet though her skills profound did smite,
The others chose the knights, despite.

For although 'Adam' did persist,
Resolute of sword and fist,
Was small and slender, pale and thin,
As 'neath her armor, dwarfed within,
The maiden struggled with her sword
As laughter 'round the tourney roared,
And so was by the knights ignored,
Preferring strong lads be their wards.

As Anabelle that e'ensong wept,
Ambition crushed, with fallen crest,
A knight in armor black as tar
Reflecting moonbeams, silver stars,
Stretched forth his arm to aid her rise,
And claim his counsel as her prize.
Though small in stature, girth and size,
'Twas fire he'd spied within her eyes.

"Your valor, child, I must commend,
But tell me, why dost thou pretend
To be a boy when thou art a girl,
As God intended in his world?"
Then spying Annabelle distraught
With furrowed brow, in turmoil caught,
The Black Knight said, "'Twas bravely fought.
To me you'll be a boy, as ought."

He pulled the child upon his steed,
Declaring, if she would agree,
To prove her daring on a quest,
And loyal, serve at his behest,
He'd make her squire, the Knight professed,
Once proven with both trial and test.

To a distant land forthwith did go
The Black Knight with his squire in tow
Where lurked a beast that must be sought
And slain afore more havoc's wrought.
Fortuitous then was the twist,
Forsooth, 'twas thought good fortune kissed
The one no other would enlist,
Sworn she to he, sword, soul and fist.

For the land where dwelled the savage sought
Was whence had come this 'lad' he'd brought;
The homeland of his trusted squire,
Whose knowledge of each stream and shire,
Of forest, hilltop, crag and mire,
The beast's entrapment would require.

Twenty throats from ear to ear
This rogue had ripped, instilling fear
Amongst the townsfolk, who did claim
There were no man, no human frame
Could drive a blade through flesh to bone
Then live amongst them as their own,
Undetected, cold as stone,
And ne'er for direst deeds atone.

Of twenty buried 'neath the ground
No limbs nor livers could be found.
Devoured, so the locals say,
By this dæmon who did slay
Victims for his evil rites,
Then feasted 'pon these grim delights;
Each body, cold and swathed with bites,
The tokens of his appetite.

Thus, Adam with the Black Knight stalked
The woodlands, glens, where evil walked,
Searching for a trace or clue
That hence forthwith might lead them to
This devil that they'd vowed to purge,
Possessed by some ungodly urge.
At night, when from his lair emerged,
They'd fight to smite this wicked scourge.

Then 4 weeks passed, 5 bodies more.
Awoken her from slumber, swore
The Black Knight to his neophyte
Upon the horrors seen that night:
"A body torn, its innards out,
Carried by one thought devout ...
The priest!" her Black Knight lord did scout
Back to his home, and had no doubt.

"Whilst tossing in my bed this eve,
Sleep bestowed but scant reprieve.
I let you rest and ventured forth
To eerie woodlands in the north,
And 'neath the full moon, there observed
The devil with his priest who served,
Dividing organs, fresh preserved
For rites of witchcraft's spells reserved!

Come, follow me," the Knight then said,
Coaxing Adam from her bed.
"We'll journey to the cottage where,
Sits he devouring flesh, and tears
Betwixt his teeth the loins and guts
Removed with disemboweling cuts.

So there, where stood the somber hut,
Shadowing the Black Knight's strut,
Adam followed, gripping hard
Her sword behind her lord, en garde,
As peering through the window, spied
The priest, his wife, their children five;
A table set upon which lay
Meat served as cutlets freshly flayed
And offal, soaked in blood, were splayed
Across each plate, a vast array.

"Could what we see be human meat,
The priest's vile brood prepare to eat?"
The apprentice said unto her lord,
The Black Knight, as unsheathed her sword.
"There is no doubt. The beast is he,"
The Black Knight said, "dost thou agree?
The organs they devour, you see,
Be tokens of his murd'rous spree!"

Adam, wrestling with her thoughts,
Piercing then the silence, fraught
By revelations mighty thrust,
Did whisper to her master, thus:
"Repressed emotions grant no peace,
So if he be both priest and beast,
With one's true hidden self released,
Carnage reigns, a bloody feast!"

Warmly, then, the Black Knight smiled;
By the wisdom of his ward beguiled,
Said, "With that, lad, this trial you've passed;
Its true intent revealed, at last.
Confused, bemused by what inside
You locked away and tried to hide
The true you, thus condemned a bride
By fools who torment, taunt and chide.
But when one's forced to masquerade,
A stranger in the skin God made,
Restrained, constrained, vile thoughts compel;
Break free now from thy private hell.
For Anabelle shall Adam quell,
Till thy beast inside doth rise as well!

'Tis justice now we both must serve,
So follow, if you have the nerve.
Wield thy sword, let vengeance reign!
May Adam's blade be Satan's bane!"

Then, breaking through the cottage door,
Her longsword through the children tore,
Their guts festooned both wall and floor,
The priest and wife sliced 2 to 4.

She plucked their hearts from out their ribs,
Still clasped inside her blood-soaked fists,
Fed the child who yet drew breath,
That clung to life and cheated death,
And made him swallow every bite
As slowly through his head she sliced
From crown to brow, his brain she diced,
His matted scalp: caked gore and lice.

And in her frenzy, Anabelle
Now Adam, chewed entrails as well;
A creature forged in fury's spell,
Her savage lust, just blood could quell,
Heard a voice demanding, "Stop!
Lay down thy sword! Pray, let it drop!"

Observing limbs sliced, diced and chopped,
And organs spliced o'er heads she'd lopped,
The Sheriff with his band of men,
Repulsed, aghast, did vomit, then
At Adam, each their blade-tip aimed,
As unto them, the 'lad' explained:
"The Black Knight, for I am his squire,
Commanded retribution dire,
With tempers burning, lust afire
For justice, thus the beast expired!

For 'twas this fiend who terrorized!
Behold, your beast: the priest, disguised!
And thus, now ends the Black Knight's quest
To rid ye of this murd'rous pest.
Yet he and I claim no reward,
Nor accolades, now victory's scored.
My valorous, black-armored lord
Appeased; well pleased with peace restored."

"Where then is this knight you serve
Who speaks not? Hath he not the nerve?
For no knight in this hut we see,
Just blood and gristle, guts and thee!"
Said Adam, pointing, "There he stands!"
Eyes following her outstretched hand,
To where the pale youth swore he stood
Saw only red-stained walls of wood.

"Come forth, my Lord," she whispered soft,
As all the sheriff's men there scoffed ...
For no knight had there ever been
But he who came one fevered dream
To Anabelle, sad, left behind,
Unto her madness, thus resigned.
The Black Knight lived where none could find,
Conjured by her fragile mind.

Epilogue:

The beast was she, for all along,
Each death she dealt, her quest prolonged,
Yet though she knew not of these wrongs,
Faint echoes hummed forgotten songs.
Each victim's gaze, both cold and stark,
Did stir a memory faint, yet dark,
Of deeds wrought in her fury's haze,
A violent trance, hypnotic daze;
Society's rejection sways;
Her burning anger set ablaze.

Thus, with her head upon the block,
Bracing for the Headsman's chop,
She gazed upon the jeering crowd;
Spied one allied, the lone head bowed.
'Twas he, her Black Knight; by his side,
A goat, black coat, horns sweeping wide,
Appeared to grin, its smile implied
With Lucifer she'd soon reside.

A knight in armor black as tar, reflecting moonbeams, silver stars,
stretched forth his arm to aid her rise and claim his counsel as her prize.

The Bear of Langoline

A minstrel's song. 14th century, Cornwall, England. The bear is likely a
metaphor for the black plague which reached England in 1348.

'Twas in the tavern when I heard the screams
As the bear arrived in Langoline
With a roar all swore could wake the dead,
It tore the arms off farmer Ned.
Then striding t'ward the square did he
Disembowel the widow Lee,
And terrified, Demdyke was clocked;
Ripped clean apart, locked in the stocks.

Then finally the beast took pause
To lick its lips and suck its claws,
And plotting what next move would be,
Through the tavern window, spied it me.
With tankard raised to gaping jaw
My eyes met his and felt the maw
Tear open flesh and bone 'gainst claw,
As set upon the prize it saw,
Ran fast and fierce t'ward the door.

To leap behind the bar, I tried,
With moral compass set aside
I punched the groom and shoved the bride
T'ward mouth she saw before she died.
And right behind the bear, in ran
The mob with pitchforks raised in hands,
But there were no match from shank or man,
Or sharpened tool of weight or brand.

He devoured the dozen trapped inside ...
The vicar Yates and groom of the bride,
But some'ow never found me hide
Behind that bar with swallowed pride.
And with its frenzy almost done,
Went back outside, and just for fun,
Caught and ripped a final one;
My eldest and unluckiest son
Bear tore in two, ere 'last he run.

And now flies buzz in Langoline
As bodies rot on the village green.
Their skin tar black and smell obscene,
Reminding all where the bear had been.

I heard talk that the mountain folk
Set traps; eight feet of vile they choked
Betwixt two trees with a stretch of rope;
Its organs with a pike they poked.
And when that bear were nearly dead
They slowly carved off half its head,
And feasted on the raw meat red;
Ground bones for flour to make their bread.

And that were all, or so thought we
Ne'er thinking nothing more could be,
As burying dead in the cemetery,
A notion then occurred to me ...
What if the beast weren't he ... but she?

For a bard reached town afore too long,
And buried in the minstrel's song
Perverse, a verse made faces long,
Beg Blessed Virgin they heard it wrong.
It spoke of a dæmon in a cave,
Its mother dead, heart full of rage,
And surely as night turns to day,
Revenge it will have when it comes of age.

For now, said song, it hibernates,
So here we sit, and drink, and wait,
Pray bear don't wake, its hunger keen,
And leave the cave on claws obscene,
Past church and stocks on the village green,
To taste the flesh in Langoline.

"And with its frenzy almost done, went back outside and just for fun,
caught and ripped a final one."

The Lycan Queen

13th century, Duchy of Brunswick-Lüneburg

A dwarf were he, not 3ft 3,
A quarter man, though handsome be.
Lost his heart to a princess fair,
He spied enthroned upon her chair,
Beside her father, a mighty King
Of all the land and everything,
Who bade each noble suitor bring
His tempered bow with tight-drawn string,
For he whose dart shall truest sing
May place upon her hand a ring.

Now, the dwarf possessed an eagle eye;
Could strike a lark mid-sky, says I!
And shoot the wings off gnats or flies
From an acre's length could if he tried.
Each shaft flew true when loosed and sprung,
But coin and title had he none,
And 3ft closer to the sun
Would serve him well, so a plot he spun.

His brother Sam were a taller man,
So in accordance with his plan,
Upon Sam's shoulders would he stand,
'Neath brother's armor, bow in hand.
At tourney then, in nobles' midst,
He donned his guise with Sam's assist,
Vowing rivals' hopes to quash,
As begging pardon for their loss,
Caught the rose the Princess tossed
T'ward Lord, entangled fates stars cross'd.

Within the hour, near all were beat;
The last of them dwarf did defeat
As 'round Sam's neck his legs clung tight,
He launched his dart with graceful flight,
And then as did the arrow land
In center mark, the crowd took stand.
As either side around him fanned,
The King bestowed his daughter's hand.

"A feast," the King declared to all,
"This night, and ere the morrow's call,
Beneath the full moon in the sky,
Our champion shall take his bride,
Then one last trial he must abide
To prove he be as we inside."

The dwarf did muse, "What test contrives
The King, to prove that deep inside
I'm like his daughter, noble-born,
Adorned in garments richly worn?
And what then of our wedding night
When faithless, telltale firelight
Reveals to her I lack the height
Of one she thinks her sturdy knight?"

 So 'fore the feast the dwarf took flight.

For 2 long years he sailed to sea,
Or 5, or 4, though some say 3,
With hopes that from his heart would flee
His love, for like her ne'er he'd be.
Then came the day an oath he swore
To steer the vessel back to shore,
And dragon's fire or serpent's roar,
Could stop not what he'd come back for,

But lo, where once the King was lord,
Now sat enthroned a sight abhorred.

The Princess once, but now the Queen
Beside a sight like none he'd seen.
A Prince chose she, near half her size
With legs like straw 'neath dwarven thighs;
More gnome than man, he did surmise,
Had passed whatever test devised
Proved worthy of her royal prize.

Each day the dwarf took to the tavern
Drowning sorrows by the flagon,
In forest, fallen from the wagon,
Stumbling through the fern and bracken,
Cursing fate that 'pon him frowned,
He spied the purple velvet gown
Of one he loved now sleeping sound
Stalked by a wolf 'top yonder mound.

The dwarf drew forth an arrow, then
Stretched bowstring back and aimed to end
Beast poised to feast and do her harm,
So resolute, with strength of arm,
Let loose a dart t'ward its eyes,
One strike to smite its swift demise.
Though brave his deed, and love survived,
Queen screamed, "Who intervened must die!"

Then seeing the dwarf, from the floor she stood,
Now calm, peeled back her velvet hood,
Decreeing folk her realm throughout
Shall celebrate their love devout.
For bravery, she would requite;
Her hand, his prize, his height despite;
This hero who the wolf did smite
Will wed her 'pon the morrow's night.

"But what of he?" dwarf said to she,
Head bowed to her on bended knee.
"A Prince you have, we can't be three!"
Her finger hushed his lips mid-plea,
Said, "Listen t'what I say to thee.
My husband died, and heart forlorn,
I ventured to these woods to mourn,
And fell asleep in fern and thorn.
Thine arrow hit, the beast lies torn,
Now unto thee my heart is sworn."

Next eve in chamber, by the fire,
The object of his heart's desire
Beckoned dwarf come through the door
From feast of wine, stuck pig, and boar;
Removed her shift that draped the floor,
With a smile that teased she wanted more.

Obliged did he, and naked be
Not eye to eye, but eye to knee,
She looked down for his girth to see,
And licking lips at one so wee,
Said, "Thought not you I'd remember thee?
My rose bestowed this archer took,
Then ran away; yet though we looked
And scoured the bounds of kingdoms vast,
To fate's command we bowed at last."
Said dwarf, "But riches had I none,
Nor size, so thought it best I run.
Afore I take thee as my bride,
Said King, his royal steed sat astride,
One final test must be applied
To prove my noble worth inside."

The Queen cast dwarf an angry glare.
"You fool," said she, "you're unaware!
That wolf you killed, didst thou suppose
A danger unto me did pose?
'Twas the Prince, my husband, killing boar,
And prowling woods in search of gore,
For when the moon is full and bright,
Those of noble birth delight,
Become like wolves and hunt at night,
Devouring peasants, slain on sight!

Your height, dwarf, it matters not,
Nor how high born, or what you've got.
The test my husband first must pass,
Is will he let me bite if asked,
And turn his shape to one like mine,
Beneath the moon, come evening time,
We'll shed our robes, cloaks, hose and dress,
And feast on bone and blood and flesh,
For the village whore, poor drunken wretch,
Shall know our hungry mouths' caress!

Your size to me meant less than naught,
But left you did, and me distraught,
And then returned to kill my mate
Thus, love professed doth come too late.
Pray Peter opens Heaven's gate
... Prepare dwarf to meet thy fate!"

And there before his widening eyes,
His love cast off her fair disguise.
With coat of hair, up straight did rise;
Her savage claws from paws grew size;
Teeth dagger-sharp, t'ward full moon cried;
The last thing seen afore he died.

Beneath the sheath of Queen's pale skin
Came forth the beast that dwells within
To tear heart's yearning limb from limb,
Rip dwarf apart from scrote to chin.

With flesh and sinew stripped and done,
No trace remained he'd been someone.
His marrow sucked and gristle gone,
She lapped whatever blood clung on;
Turned human 'pon the dawning sun
As swarming flies bred maggot young.

Then t'ward the dwarven bones she'd gnawed
'Neath full moon, strewn across the floor,
She tossed a rose, like one before
She gave a Lord whose arrows scored,
Possessed her heart, then fled the shore
Before a bite she could accord,
And like her, lead their Lycan horde.

True love eternal, his reward.

"With flesh and sinew stripped and done,
no trace remained he'd been someone."

Bleat, Bleat, the Black Goat

The nursery rhyme *Baa, Baa, Black Sheep* was first published in the year 1490 in the book *Compendium Fabularum Maleficarum Pueris*, a collection of children's stories concerning witchcraft and the occult, under its original title: *Bleat, Bleat, the Black Goat*. Written in Latin, it contained eighteen verses which, thankfully, have been edited down over the centuries to the essential singular verse we are familiar with today. The reason why will become glaringly obvious after reading the earliest known version, presented here for your soon-to-be displeasure.

It was purportedly translated into English by William Caxton, publisher of Chaucer's *Canterbury Tales* and the first person in England to print books using a printing press. He died shortly thereafter. Today, only three copies of the *Compendium* are known to exist in private collections (one being my own). It is worth noting that one of these three copies was owned by Anton LaVey, renowned devil-worshiper and author of *The Satanic Bible*, and was purchased from his estate following his death. The whopping $1.2 million price it fetched at auction from an anonymous buyer can be attributed less to the rarity of the book itself and more to the curious inscription inside the jacket of LaVey's copy, which read:

"*Anton, In perpetuum, frater, ave atque vale* (Forever and ever, brother, hail and farewell). *Until we meet again, LFR.*"

Although the identity of 'LFR' remains a mystery, some believe the book was a gift from LaVey's dark master ... the devil himself.

Baa, Baa, the Black Sheep,
Hast thou any wool?
Yes sire, yes sire,
Three sacks full.
One is for the master,
And one is for his bride;
Another for the fair dame who down the lane resides.

Cluck, Cluck, the Black Hen,
Canst thou lay an egg?
Yes sire, yes sire,
'Tis only one you beg?
For lo, in the straw
Are seven more I laid,
So prithee, fill thy basket and feed me corn to trade.

Moo, Moo, the Black Cow,
Thy milk shall quench my thirst.
Yes sire, yes sire,
Afore you drain me, first
Rub thy hands together,
Pray touch me when they're warm,
And shoo away the vexing flies that 'round my udder swarm.

Neigh, Neigh, the Black Horse,
Wilt thou let me ride?
Yes sire, yes sire,
Pray, sit my back astride.
I'll trot and I'll canter,
And o'er the fields I'll run,
So hold on tightly to my mane and let us have our fun.

Oink, Oink, the Black Pig,
'Tis pork from thee I seek.
Yes sire, yes sire,
My hocks, or rump, or cheek?
Pray, lead me to the butcher,
So I may know his blade,
And sweet ham wilt thou feast upon once I meet the grave.

Bleat, Bleat, the Black Goat,
Might I touch your horns?
Yes sire, yes sire,
Pray, why art thou forlorn?
You've three sacks of black wool,
Cow's milk, and a lamb,
You galloped 'pon a horse's back,
And feast on eggs and ham.

Aye, Aye, Black Goat,
My pain thou hast perceived.
No home have I, no friends, nor coin;
An orphan girl I be.
I bartered with the Black Sheep
Three bags of wool to trade,
Inside of one I hid a lamb, and then its mother flayed.

I took eggs from the Black Hen
And corn for these did vow,
But as it pecked, I wrung its neck,
Then ran to find the Cow.

I drained the Cow for jollies
For milk I do not like,
But beef or steak, I'll gladly take,
So carved it with my knife.

'Twas then I rode the Black Horse
Too hard, till lame it fell.
Then as it lay and neighed in pain,
I killed that nag as well.

The Black Pig then I butchered,
No whetstone did I own.
My blade was blunt; it squealed and grunted,
Sliced from skin to bone.

Tsk, Tsk, thy Black Heart,
Evil thou hast been.
Now wouldst thou like to travel
To the realms thy heart hath dreamed?
Sign the book before thee;
I will guide thy hand,
And unto thee shall grant a power few can understand.

Tarry, Tarry, Black Goat,
What wilt thou from me
To know the taste of butter,
And to live deliciously?
For if it is my soul thou want'st,
Then willingly I give,
And happ'ly ever after in thy service I shall live!

——————— ———— ——————

Baa, Baa, the Black Sheep,
Hast thou wool to spare?
Nay sirs, nay sirs,
The orphan stripped me bare.
And where be this orphan?
For she shall know our fists!
This child did steal a lamb,
Then killed the cow, horse, hen and pig!

Nay, Nay, ye Silly Fools,
Best ye bind thy tongues,
Or she'll add them too, into her brew,
And eyeballs, just for fun.

Seek her in the forest yon
If ye have the nerve;
Casting charms to do us harm,
The Black Goat's will to serve.

So Pray, Pray, Ye Children
Her soul might still be saved,
And burn not in the lake of fire
When cast into the grave.

For yes, she wears the pretty dress,
And powers doth possess,
But damned will be those chosen
To receive his black caress.

Eternally shall roast all folk
Who suckle 'pon his breasts.

Seek her in the forest yon if ye have the nerve;
Casting charms to do us harm, the Black Goat's will to serve.

Gelfred and The Vampyr

1393, Duchy of Mecklenburg-Stargard. Author unknown. Predating Polidori's *The Vampyre* by more than 400 years, it is possibly the earliest example of vampire fiction known to exist.

Gelfred, self-assured and strong
Set forth upon a journey long,
His fortune on this quest to find,
With trials to test his strength and mind.
And should he deem a maiden fair
A worthy bride to bear his heir,
Freely, would his heart surrender,
Thus, bravely through the mountains ventured.

In a village far he rested his feet,
And sought a tavern for to eat.
Devoured sausage, bread of rye,
Honey mead and chicken thigh;
Then with his thirst and hunger stilled,
He journeyed onward, purpose filled,
But though the hour was nearly noon,
O'erhead the sun lay veiled in gloom;
'Pon yonder bluff a castle loomed,
Its shadow cast did all entomb
Like some foreboding, fearsome womb;
Dread omen of impending doom.

Of the tavern wench, he did inquire,
"What noble, baron, king or squire
Occupies that fortress there
Which shadows all from sunlight's glare?
'Tis nearly noon yet seems like night.
It hides all from day's rays of light,
That none in sun may take delight;
In truth, the sight doth give me fright!"

Said wench, "Beware and keep thee clear.
Pray, stray not from the path nor veer,
For cursed things lurk within those walls,
And any fool who ventures falls.
For with the beast that there resides,
We forged a pact all must abide,
Thus, none from here may go inside,
Nor others with a curious eye;
Shouldst thou be tempted to defy,
We'll strike by troth, for if you try,
One breaks the oath, then ten will die!"

"What creature in this castle dwells
That traps ye in its fearful spell?
In the art of swordplay none compare;
I'll storm the heights with blade laid bare,
And once within the walls do swear
To purge what scourge awaits me there!"

'Pon Gelfred gazed the wench and laughed,
"Go forth and through this village pass;
Pray no more questions of me ask.
Many like thee there have been,
Count stones in graveyard ... seventeen.
All climbed up to the mountain top,
This devil thought with ease they'd stop,
Its throat to slice and head to lop,
Yet once inside the gates they dropped.

Though fate hath marked thee noble bred
With deadly hands, as thou hast said,
No blade or pike nor arrow's head
... Can kill what be already dead."

Her words caused Gelfred's jaw to drop.
Frozen, rooted to the spot,
Said, "None in God's creation be
As this thou hast described to me!"

Then through yon door the preacher came;
Beheld a sight seen ere again,
All seventeen, no life or name,
'Neath gravestones lay, this one the same,
If wisdom fails to cool pride's flame.

Said the preacher, "Sir, I tell thee plain,
Thy fanciful flight thy might restrain,
This fiend deemed fit to draw thine aim
Delights as daylight's shadows wane,
'Tis a Nosferatu, none dare name,
A thing once dead yet lives again!

It drinks warm blood to stay alive
By ways the Devil himself devised!
I'll tell thee now how we survive;
All living here shun fear and thrive ...

When five years pass, 'tis then decreed
Our fairest bloom to it we cede.
This virgin maiden thus we send
And nevermore do see again
Our sinless lamb of sacrifice,
In wolfsbane, clove, and edelweiss
Adorned, and mourned, dark Lord enticed,
Her blameless blood, the Vampyr's price.

And in return, it stalks us not;
No longer seeking blood it sought,
With belly full, the monster pleased,
Its foul desires are thus appeased;
Five years thenceforth we live at ease.

This wretched one, protect do we
From glory seekers such as thee,
Whose brawn outmatched by lack of smarts
Upsets the steady apple cart.
'Tis evil few have e'er conceived,
And broken oaths our peace upheaves,
Thus, lest thy sweetheart be bereaved,
Sir, sup thine ale and take thy leave!"

Undaunted by these warnings told,
With sword held firm, assured and bold,
O'er battlements that very night,
Guided by the full moon's light,
To kill what Christian faith abhors;
Portcullis breached, then through the ward;
His gaze set firm and fate ignored,
Spied Gelfred then, the Vampyr Lord!

Taking pause to weigh his plight
His eyes beheld this ghastly sight.
Stood the Vampyr, twenty hands in height,
Cold eyes ablaze that pierced the night;
Red lips like scars 'cross sallow white
Framed needle smile's beguiled delight.

Spying Gelfred, it paused, and from its chin
Wiped blood, as bared its dreadful grin,
But judged was not the boy for his sin
Of breaching the walls and sneaking in.
'Stead bade him forth t'ward the door
With a finger's razor-sharp arced claw,
To brave the lair none before
Had lived to tell what horrors saw.

This pest, possessed; a force malign.
The offer dared he not decline;
Still leery of the beast's designs,
Stepped forth inside its cursèd shrine,
But saw he not to Christ divine
A vile affront, nor pagan sign,
But style that spoke of taste refined;
A fire stoked, cup filled with wine,
Before a table set to dine.

Like a gracious host without reserve
Called servants forth to tend and serve.
Thought Gelfred: courtesy deceives,
With wine it puts my mind at ease
For sly kill's thrill; a devil's tease.

As ice on fire the Vampyr spoke,
"Pray fear not boy, for by my troth
To kill is not my aim, you see
Thy thoughts hear I, as I were thee.
So if thou think'st to strike a blow
Before thy blade be drawn, I'll know,
And like the others, thou wilt go
Where maggots feast in graves below.

For on this night, thou art my guest;
None do I have, nor do request,
And die who try when care I less;
Their doom is writ at my behest.
But once or twice each century,
I crave a mortal's company,
And the fearless soul that drives thy cause
Reminds me of what once I was.

Handsome, strong, of noble birth,
And brave as thee when born to earth,
But alas, chose not my lover well;
To netherworlds her spirit fell.
Her soul's eternal rest denied,
The shadowed realm 'twixt death and life
She walked; her flesh, decay defied,
For human blood did thirst to thrive.

Afraid to live beyond my breath,
She kissed my vein; 'twas fatal gift,
The dread undead, by shadows chained;
Condemned to live fate's dark refrain.

'Twas with my gift to her of blood
That bound us in eternal love,
Till death did claim her, 'neath the sun,
A Vampyr's skin like fire becomes.
Alone here now, years sixty score,
Her face forgotten, behind these doors,
Cursed, I live forever more."

From Gelfred came a stern reply:
"No pity for your words have I.
I'd wager where the gloom resides,
Is where you chain these virgin brides,
And maidens sent here unto thee
Like moths to flame, their fates shall be!"

The Vampyr shook his head and smiled,
"To falsehoods thou hast reconciled.
These village girls that stir thy speech,
Deem doomed, consumed; their endings bleak,
Now English, French, and Latin speak;
Each yearning heart its want doth seek.

With manners, grace, and learned minds,
A world beyond their dreams they find,
Then land and riches I bestow,
So a life of comfort each might know.
Thus, those perceived I apprehend,
To the finest schools I justly send;
'Tis this way hate abates and mends
And saves them from fate's squalid end.

Wouldst know how such a beast as I,
Bereft of blood yet stays alive?
A bargain with each girl I make,
Two things thus in return must take.
The first: unyielding loyalty
From each, for opportunity;
I crowned them all with majesty,
And forged their will to serve but me.
Should danger then upon me fall,
Through veil of night and spectral pal,
Across all realms they rise at call
To wreak their vengeance, each and all."

"You spake, Vampyr, of favors two;
What more are they required to do?"
Quoth the Vampyr, "'Pon thee I bestow
No deeper secret that I know.
A flask of blood to pay the fee,
Drawn fresh from veins, o'er land and sea
Doth travel swift and secretly
Hither, 'tis their Lord's decree.

Each year comes food they freely give,
And nourished thusly, so I live.
Though never can my soul be saved,
In such a way, these lives well made
Repay mankind for those I've slayed."

Though fear and intrigue both took hold,
As the Vampyr's dreadsome tale was told,
Foul stench that idle talk enfolds
Smelled Gelfred like death's rotting mold.
For those whose hearts true evil breeds
Inherently do wicked deeds.
Though granted opportunities,
Embroiled in spoils and luxuries,
He shuns the possibility
These maidens all lived happily,
And torn from kin, will not concede
'Tis sin that childless mothers grieve;
To saints and Blessed Virgin plead.

Hence, by confessions of his own,
A thousand years or more hath known,
And the lives he's taken for that long
Be a vast, unnamed, forsaken throng.
Vowed Gelfred then to right this wrong.

His inner thoughts the beast could hear.
Aware, with stealth and care, did steer
Events, with ill intent unclear,
He bravely spoke to cloak his fear.

"Vampyr, 'spite thy ceaseless cries,
Unable art thou still to die.
If thy true intent is not to live,
Perhaps assistance I can give
To bring end to this wanton spell
And damn thy soul where evil dwells?"

The Vampyr laughed, "Try as thou might,
With wings of a bat I'll take to flight,
And with the strength of twenty men
I'll pluck thy limbs like petals, then
With sharper teeth than raven claws,
I'll tear thy throat; on flesh I'll gnaw,
Ere sword from scabbard canst thou draw,
Thus fatal be thy favor's flaw!"

Said Gelfred, "Wretch! No sword I need
To send thee back to hell with speed.
Our conversation long hath been;
Beyond the window, yet unseen,
The sun ascends, the night retreats,
With heaven's light I'll have thee beat!
No maids nor men then shalt thou eat!"
He shouted, jumping from his seat.

Then, leaping t'wards where daylight hides
'Neath ornate tapestry's rear side,
He tore the curtain down mid-flight
The moment dawn usurped the night.
Till judgment's fire consumed the room,
As sunlight sealed the Vampyr's doom!

Amidst the flames, the creature smiled,
As to its fate it reconciled,
Yet why it burned and battled not
A clue within its gaze was caught.
To hell, its dark soul did descend,
And greeted there as Satan's friend,
Though truly evil, thus condemned,
The Vampyr's tale had yet to end.

Four years forward from that night,
To wealthy Gelfred gave delight,
A noble maiden, pure, snow white,
Did she, with he, love's vows recite:
"Let no man part what God unites."

As Gelfred sang good fortune's song,
He made with her three children strong.
Her dowry unto him bestowed
A family fortune and chateau,
With vineyard, hence to France did go
For blessed seeds of grapes to sow.

And thus, a merry life they made,
Until one evening with a blade,
Inside their chamber, Gelfred spied
To cut her vein, his Lady tried,
So desperate, unto her, he cried:

"Beloved, stop! Desist! Refrain!
Remove the dagger from thy vein!
For if death is thy true design,
The next life for thy knife is mine!
What joy have I that fails to share?
What anguish caused have I to bear,
That thou wouldst end thy days so fair?
I pray thee cease this dark despair!"

'Twas then that Gelfred spied the flask,
Which, when she had fulfilled the task,
Would catch her blood,
Though loath to ask,
Implied this act be not her last;
His love's kept secret plot, unmasked.

As Gelfred watched her from the door
Her smile was one seen once before
On the Vampyr's face, betwixt the flames,
When fire his wretched soul reclaimed.
Soft fawning voice to him explained:

"My love, this I do secretly;
What none must know, I tell to thee.
Long ago, my family poor
Gave up their child to a wealthy Lord.
And though this Lord all loathed, despised,
Deplored, he who hath hell baptized,
Did teach me wit and make me wise,
And saved me from a poor demise.

This pauper's daughter none would mourn,
Did train amongst the higher-born,
With manners, books, silk dresses worn,
Unto a Lady, I transformed.
Taught poise and noble etiquette,
My humble ways did soon forget.
Took gift of dowry, noble name;
A chateau with a fortune came;
Vaults filled with gold, I hold the keys,
Land with meadows, streams, and trees,
'Round castle, far as eyes can see,
The boundless gifts bound unto me.

But such a life doth bear a price;
My blood spilled, flask filled, will suffice.
For though my Lord ne'er did me harm,
Cursed was he by Satan's charm.
A Nosferatu he became;
A beast once buried, walks again!
I draw from veins to pay the wage,
Then bid depart my trusted page,
And once delivered, blood by troth
Pays in part my sacred oath.
For something more my Lord requires ...
Revenge 'pon one who did conspire
To end his reign with flames of fire.
For the wicked knave brought forth the pyre,
Consequences shall be dire!"

Disbelieving ears and eyes,
Said Gelfred, "Why hast thou disguised
This secret so? Are we not wed?
'Tis not a fact thy Lord lies dead?
And thus expired, when the killer is found,
How can he plot from 'neath the ground,
To slay the knave who cut him down?"

The Lady quoth, "Whose deed this be,
A hero then became, for he,
By killing that which all men feared,
Was hailed and loved; by all revered.
Folk sang and danced, brought forth was cheer
Till wintertide that very year ...

There came a plague and half were done,
Then followed drought and scorching sun;
With failing crops came famine's blight
And those still breathing thought they might
Be stricken by the Vampyr's curse;
The one drains veins with fevered thirst
Seeks retribution for their crimes;
Dark vengeance wrought of Lord maligned!

So on to the castle, empty and cold,
Went all to see how death took hold,
And though 'twas fire caused Lord's dispatch,
His charred heart lay amongst the ash.
Thus, with our blood and ashes twined,
Soon our Lord new life shall find,
For our pact requires that each one give
Her secret gift so he may live.

With blood, resolve, tenacity,
His coven serves; nine bound that be,
Who swore undying loyalty,
And unto him owe fealty,
Will search this earth, both land and sea
Till stones unturned, none shall there be.

When comes the day this knave is found,
We'll steal away, his body bound;
Beaten, blinded, forced to kneel
Before our Lord, his wrath to feel.
And should thereby his kin we find,
With flesh to scourge and bones to grind,
To the dungeons be they all confined;
Their warm blood drained for him to dine!"

His Lady gazed 'pon Gelfred stern,
"Go!" said she, "my secret's learned!
From knowledge comes no swift return.
If for my love thy heart still yearns,
Pray, help me find and aid me burn
He who hath my life upturned.
No longer can this cut adjourn ...
By duty bound, I fill this urn!"

As he took his leave and the stairs ascended,
Knew Gelfred his life that night had ended.
For soon his wife would come to loathe
And shun the one 'pon love bestowed.
For the sacred oath she swore, ordained
She'd take him to her Lord in chains,
And yield their children's blood to drain
To glut him on their crimson veins.

Thus, high atop the castle walls,
As Gelfred's tragic tale recalls,
He brought two children, babe and all,
And found loose bricks to bear their fall.
He cast them down t'ward the ground,
Then leapt himself; whilst falling down,
Recalled a preacher once did say:
"Sup up thine ale and walk away,"
Yet from such counsel went astray,
Thus came he to his dying day.

Though blood not drawn, and fall he may,
Still Gelfred was the Vampyr's prey.

On the Subject of Cats

Origins and date are unknown.

Kindly be unto a cat,
When seeing one, avoid a spat
That causes harm and suffering,
Or the same in kind upon thee bring.

Knot not its tail with rope nor twine,
The other end bind to a swine,
So pig and cat play tug-of-war.
As screams the cat with hind legs sore,
Contrives it a way to even the score.

Throw a cat in water, then thou shalt see
Few beasts abide such enmity.
Avenging thus this wicked act,
Coiled, it boils and plots attack,
For tenfold will it pay thee back.

To kick it too hath consequence,
And a cat shall seek its recompense;
Revenge in kind for a deed most foul,
Though cowering 'neath thy trembling cowl
Shan't stop the cat's chastising scowl
Or gentle purr defer to growl.

For the cat, prepare a sacrifice
Of milk from goat, or meat from mice,
And hope these offerings suffice,
As rightful penance for thy vice.

But should the feline not forgive,
Be mindful how thou ought'st to live.
Look close, peer deep behind its eyes,
Its spirit's lived a thousand lives,
Observing every move we make,
All those we love and oft forsake,
Each mead-swayed deed we dare partake;
Sworn oaths by troth, tap-shackled, break.
All that we've done, did, gone, and been,
Each prayer or wanton act obscene,
Reveals the cat to ghosts unseen;
From cats, our sins the spirits glean.

Visiting the neighbors, hence,
When sleeping sound, these ghosts commence
To whisper wicked hearsay heard,
Till neighbors wake to spread the word
About thee, thus with haste they go
To taverns, as the rumors grow
Where flagons flow as gossip weaves
And slander's tangled web deceives.

Till all in the village know thy dirt ...
What wench with lust did seek to flirt;
On which soft cheek there sprouts a boil;
How hands were slathered soft with oil,
As wife at home with babies toiled,
To spill thy seed, 'fore hard recoiled.
Though 'hard' length of a finger be
Between thy legs, too wee to see,
With hardly length enough to pee!

How wife did catch thee in the act,
So 'pon thy back with a lash she cracked,
And flogging, chased thee down the street
For milking thus, thy tiny meat.

And hearing this, the tavern laughs
At the beating took for tugging thy shaft.
A laughing stock thou shalt become,
And all because thy soul was numb
To the plight of a cat, so prithee, be kind;
Be soft of heart and sound of mind.

If e'er a cat should cross thy path,
Heed well its gaze and silent wrath.
A vessel it might be for a witch,
Whose spirit with this feline switch'd.

Its yellow, piercing eyes enchant
To bid thee serve as its servant;
To see its whims and will be done,
Thus cursèd live; its slave become,
And all because one rainy day,
Cruelly, thou didst chase away
From fire's hearth, a shivering cat,
Where sheltering from the storm it sat.
Thy belly full, refused to feed
Cat scraps of fowl or sips of mead.
Now harken friend, be shrewd, take heed,
No blessings bloom from spiteful deeds.
Who wakes the ire of feline breeds,
Shall stoke the fire of dæmon seeds!

Yet every tale reveals a way
Where fate may turn should one but stray,
For no vile end shalt thou abide
With a cat companion by thy side.

Evading gossip, wagging tongues,
When thou and she as ward are one.
As soft caresses of her fur
Reward thee with a calming purr,
A human mate for life she'll choose,
Affection given, love ensues,
But leery be thee of thy muse.

For men whose minds outsize a rat's,
For reasons thus, steer clear of that
Which leads to a quarrel, row, or spat
With a foe as worthy as the cat!

Dedicated to my own cat, Balerion the Dread, to celebrate
the joy she hath brought to my life after first being kindly
unto her.

The Princess and the Puppet Maker

Adapted from the fairytale *Griezelwürst der Puppenmaker* (1491) by Waldemar Eutener, scribe to Frederick I, Margrave of Brandenburg-Ansbach, and his wife Sophia of Poland, written for their children should correction or unusual punishment be so required.

The Enchantment and the Meeting

In days of yore when hunger reigned and death was in the air,
There lived a man with nimble hands and cold enchanted stare.
His dolls would pace with lifelike grace upon the cobbled square,
And whispers spoke of stolen souls that lingered, hidden there.

This fellow's name was Griezelwürst, a man of some renown,
For legends of his dolls and puppets spread beyond the town,
And noble houses, near and far, would seek to buy his wares,
For none with craft and cunning in the kingdom's bounds compared.

Die Gelbe Angst, dubbed *the Yellow Dread,* was rife throughout the land,
So Saturday, upon the stroke of noon, each week, as planned,
Griezelwürst would entertain; his marionettes beguiled,
To gift the poor respite from woes, if only for a while.

Word reached the king of Griezelwürst, his craft and talents rare,
And so unto the palace summoned was the master where
The king commanded for the princess no expense be spared
On a show like none before had known; to Griezelwürst declared:

Your finest dolls and marionettes like none have ever seen,
Engaged upon the royal stage, each face and figurine
Carved with such precision that my court will scarce believe
The sight before their eyes that night, which none hath e'er perceived.

But most of all, the princess, my beloved one, no less,
Is who your crafted, dancing, wooden wonders must impress.
For this shall be her father's gift upon her birthday's eve.
Ten bags of gold, your payment, should this wonder be achieved."

And with a deep and grateful bow, Herr Griezelwürst agreed.

For hours he toiled, both day and night; food and sleep he shunned,
Creating such a grand delight, the like seen ne'er by none.
When came the night his dolls took flight, unburdened by their wires,
Aghast, all those at the court did ask what magic had conspired

To bring about a wonder thus, so lifelike, could a man
Carve wood with such precision, spawn this wonder from his hands?
Stepped forward then the princess royal, enraptured by the sights
And sounds, as smiled, beguiled by what she'd witnessed there that night.

Then as her eyes met Griezelwürst's, her heart inside her chest
Did beat as though ten thousand drummers drummed at love's behest,
And smitten too was Griezelwürst, enraptured by the sight
Of the princess royal, for whom he'd toiled, who stole his heart that night.

As though enchanted by a spell, he bowed, she bid him stand,
And placed a gentle kiss upon his cheek, and he her hand.
Then as her lips did part, imparting truth that 'neath her breast,
Her heart did pound, with love resounding wantonly, professed.

"'Tis late," the king did state and bade the puppet maker leave,
Promising that gold upon the morrow he'd receive.
For spied had he his daughter and the puppet maker's gaze,
And marked the shadowed fire of lust their mingling set ablaze.

The Wrath of the King

Now, Griezelwürst was patient, for composure and restraint
Are traits that bless a craftsman with the sufferance of a saint,
But when the weeks turned into months and payment never came,
A craftsman too will turn, 'tis true, when guile fans anger's flame.

So to the palace gates each morning Griezelwürst would go,
Demanding gold the king did hold as payment for his show.
But ne'er would he relent; the king's intent to strike a blow
To one who lit his daughter's fire, his bitter ire would know!

Petitioning the Church, the king unto the bishop claimed
Unholy magic was the reason for the craftsman's fame,
"For how else but by witchcraft could his puppets seem alive?
By skill or luck, or deals struck with the devil?" he contrived.

"Thy lack of proof to prove the truth," said bishop to the king,
"Saves Griezelwürst from fire, or worse; his favor, fate doth swing.
Departed souls placed into dolls? 'Tis folly, that you speak!
This man accused of such a ruse is not the fiend you seek!"

The king knew well the spell the master wove o'er hearts of all,
And beggars, whores, to highborn lords would nary see him fall.
Now the Church refused to burn him, lest they face the people's wrath,
So plotting Griezelwürst's demise, he strolled a darker path ...

The Betrayal

With an appetite for spite, the king forbad each noble lord
From buying that which Griezelwürst would craft, lest face the sword.
And guards outside the puppet shop prevented passersby,
Hearts set upon a marionette, from venturing too nigh.

For those who sought a puppet, and dared his will defy,
Faced pikes to poke, a rope to choke and blades to blind an eye.
Till came the night from then to when The Watchman met the king.
Genuflected, bowed; an urgent message he did bring:

"My Palace Watch hath spied the princess sneaking past the gates,
To a tiny puppet shop in town, where her lover waits.
These rendezvous, if rumor's true, and whispers are sincere,
Have been occurring since the night they met; what's more, I fear,

Possessed by their desires, conspire both lovers to escape
And flee far from the kingdom." Stood the king, his mouth agape.
Determined that his daughter ne'er again should set her eyes
Upon this curse, Herr Griezelwürst, the wretched and despised!

Destitute, poor Griezelwürst now barely had a crust,
Yet still performed each Saturday for all, as felt he must.
Beseeching him for grace, the princess begged her father stop,
But when the king refused to yield, that night unto the shop

She fled and stayed till dawn, then 'pon the morn, she took her leave.
An eve beside her lover lent her sorrow scant reprieve.
Soon word did reach the king, once more his daughter had defied.
Restrained by chains, he locked the princess in a tower high.

And there she'd stay, hid well away, until his plans took flight,
So an army of his starving subjects dined as kings that night,
And then the purse owed Griezelwürst, one hundred bags of gold,
He paid unto the common folk, whose will he now controlled.

Then in the square, next Saturday, as Griezelwürst beguiled,
Poor folk who once forgot their troubles for a while and smiled,
As puppets danced and leaped and pranced, the artist now reviled
Was mocked and gibed by souls the bribe of royal gold defiled.

The master struck by muck they chucked did run, as 'pon him rained
Stale bread and dung, what shit still clung to privy pots they drained.
Then gazing o'er his shoulder saw his puppets put to flame.
His shop ablaze, his life's work razed, as bid *Auf Wiedersehen.*

The puppet maker's wrath, thenceforth, could never more be tamed.

Mysterious Muffins

A year then passed; those there, when asked what happened on the night
They set ablaze the master's dolls and drove him from their sight,
Said little of the travesty, though others quietly claimed
They heard faint shrieks and squeaks of torment rising from the flames.

And lips would purse when Griezelwürst was mentioned, thus his name
'Cross land and sea was ne'er to be an utterance again.
At pain of death, no whispered breath his innocence professed;
Tarred and feathered, tethered, any a foolish tongue confessed.

Starvation wrought the kingdom; though they sought to thwart the *Dread,*
Still, carts did line the streets, a penny paid to take the dead.
And seldom was the king e'er seen yond palace walls' confines,
As the princess, locked inside the tower, for her lover pined.

Till one day, as their hunger raged and nearly brought them down,
Heralds far and wide proclaimed, by edict of the crown,
That every man and wife with child should rally to the court,
For the king had food arriving in a fortnight at the port!

A deal was struck with lands afar to end their hunger's burn,
Yet the kingdom that endowed the gift sought something in return.
Threatened by a war and short of able men, their plight.
Thus, every boy must sail and with their army learn to fight.

Each daughter, too, should do her part, thus each girl must enlist,
Sewing tunics, feeding mouths as long as would persist
The threat of doom that did consume their people, thus agreed
Reluctantly, to send their babes, all starving did concede.

When came the day a ship made port, filled bow to stern with food,
The starving masses lined the dock, all those that sent their brood
Of girls and boys, who sailed to sea as payment for their bread,
But what unloaded from the hull was something else instead …

Muffins, stuffed, each shape and size; delicious was the taste.
Salty, sweet, 'twere meat or beet? For no one quite could place.
No crumb was spared, no morsel lost, no scrap was cast to waste;
Though joy was found, a hidden cost each eager mouth embraced.

And every week a new supply arrived without delay,
Sustaining life, curtailing strife; the *Dread* kept well at bay.
Though happy was the kingdom, their minds, content, did stray,
And pondered oft their children, hunger forced them send away.

Griezelwürst's Revenge

When naught was heard, no bird, nor word, the mob had one intent:
Entreat their king, scarce seen, to offer mercy and relent.
Were their babes in schools or graves? Their children forth they sent,
Weighed heavy on their hearts; by night their dreams would oft torment.

Pushing past the gates and guards, the crowd did shout and jeer,
As gathered in the throne room, on the throne, the king appeared.
And hearing every grievance, every outrage and offense,
The king just smiled and bade them go back where they came from whence.

"For every child this night returns; now sleeping in their beds,
Wrapped in blankets, warm and safe ... 400 happy heads!
No war they fought, well fed, each brought us time when all near fell,
But now our kinder grace these shores, all joyous, fit and well!"

The peasants gaped in marvelment, amazed and wide of eyes;
For the very eve they sought reprieve drew forth their awed surprise.
Then as they bowed to hurry home, 'twas then the cobbler spied:
Suspended was the king by string; to silken thread was tied!

A hush fell o'er the crowd as slowly, whispers turned to cries,
As all assembled saw the wires and finally realized
Their king was just a marionette; a doll in monarch's guise.
Its wooden limbs that creaked and swayed betrayed the truth inside.

The king's enmeshed, green molding flesh they found within its shell,
With wires and fobs, small gears and cogs; all gathered there could tell
The one reviled, cast from the land, whose legend still endured,
Could fashion such a vessel to exact revenge, had lured

The people to the palace, for they too had done him wrong,
Destroying all his hands did craft; the taunting, hateful throng
Had sold their souls for bags of gold; his kindness had betrayed.
What recompense would Griezelwürst demand of them be paid?

Rampaging through the palace, the people struck with fright
Disarmed the guards and to the highest tower went that night;
And there, the princess in her prison moved not from her bed,
For like the king with strings, there lay a puppet in her stead!

And seeing this, the peasant-folk, struck by terror, said:

"Let us now back to our homes, for there our children wait!"
But Griezelwürst's cruel retribution too did seal their fate,
For in each bed a painted head, perverted by what pain
Cast mouths agape to twist in shape; from eyeballs tears did rain.

Each one a doll, carved in the image of a girl or boy
Their 'king on strings' decreed they bring, for 'twas the master's ploy
They'd ship their children 'cross the sea unto an island where
He'd bake them into muffins in the ovens of his lair,

Then send them back so all could feed; delicious was the taste.
Salty, sweet, 'twas meat not beet, this texture none could place.
The princess, now his wife, assisted with the ghastly deed
Of grinding bones to flour; baking flesh on which they'd feed.

'Twas Griezelwürst's design she'd flee the palace to his side,
Then to the king send forth a puppet in his daughter's guise.
Imprisoned in the tower, ne'er the king did realize;
Then killing him, encased within a marionette, devised

His plan for retribution, now prepare to be surprised ...

The Doll Shop

Late at night, by candle light, the master in his place,
Traced final touches with a brush upon a puppet's face.
Quick nibble of his muffin, placing cotton in his ears,
To quell the screams of children's tortured wails and sobbing tears.

Beneath him in the basement, the ovens' fires were stoked,
To bake the few remaining children vengeance hath provoked.
Up the staircase comes his wife, and whispers from the door,
"Our little muffins bake, my love. But soon, we must find more."

Amongst the cries, a wry and vengeful smile did cross his face,
But in its arc, 'tis something stark that strikes as out of place:
Unnatural twitches of his hand, as though compelled by gears,
A mechanism that predates a timepiece by some years.

Griezelwürst, himself a doll, had been so since the *Dread*
Consumed him when impoverished and sustained by crusts of bread.
With assistance of the princess royal, to whom he taught the art
Of placing souls within the confines of a puppet's heart,

He lives to love eternally, and when her time draws near,
The princess too shall pass into a puppet that appears
To be alive, as there inside, forevermore her soul
With Griezelwürst's, her love, the puppet master in control.

The Endless Woe

A cart trails through the streets of town, in a kingdom cold and gray,
For the *Yellow Dread* had spread soon aft their children went away.
The townsfolk gaunt, as though enchanted, clamor for their prize:
Muffins baked from body parts, relied on yet despised.

Little wooden dolls there dance where once their children played,
And torn hearts still perpetuate this sad, grotesque charade.
Beleaguered by disease and strife, too weary to resist,
The people line and dine upon the babes they once did kiss.

As one aggrieved retrieves his muffin, o'er the place he stood,
He catches sight of one familiar glancing 'neath a hood,
Sitting 'pon the cart and smiling at the puppet show,
Pulling strings of those he's torn, that ne'er a thread can sew.

With those who wronged him trapped within an endless reel of woe,
Griezelwürst, the Puppet Maker, onward then did go ...

Author's Note: Purportedly, the author of this piece, Waldemar Eutener, was himself an aspiring marionettist. Fragmentary records held in the archives of the Franconian court suggest that he succumbed to madness in his later years, believing himself to be the very protagonist of his own tale. Among the several unsettling curiosities uncovered in his home following his death was a vast oven, secreted away in the cellar—an object which, according to a now-missing inventory list, was *gefüllt mit Asche und kleinen Knochen—* filled with ash and small bones.

The King, The Castle,
The Bishop, and The Boy

12th century, Kingdom of Poland. Originally published in the collection, *Opowieści o Rycerzach i Koszmarach* (Tales of Knights and Nightmares)

A noble lad, pale, frail, and weak,
Short of limb and hollow cheek'd,
Feeble, was both thin and meek,
With voice soft as a mouse's squeak.

By parents, he was less adored;
O'er daughter, their affections poured.
Too thin to lift a mace or sword,
Was thus by all at court ignored.

To his father, the King, all bent the knee,
A master, he, of strategy.
No battles had his armies lost;
All flayed, those made to count the cost
Are peeled if they refuse to yield;
Their corpses strew the battlefield.

Whilst knowing that he'd never lose,
Another heir he sought to choose,
For his sickly son lacked strength and will,
And cried if but a fly he'd kill.

His daughter he proclaimed successor,
Akin, like him a born aggressor.
Vowed in his stead she'd take his throne,
Though rightful heir, his son disowned,
Bored, ignored, the sad lad roamed.

As the King one evening took his rest
A din outside became a pest.
A rider shouting, 'pon a horse,
Rode steadfast, brave, did stay the course
With a message for his King to read,
Its dire warning for to heed.

Said knight, "'Tis far I've come, my liege,
For a castle had we under siege
Till dawn upon the fourteenth day,
For sure 'twere witchcraft, all there say!
One hundred men have disappeared,
Leaving shields and swords and spears.
Four legions slept the night before,
Yet 'pon the morrow were no more!"

So spake the King, "You come this day
With news of cowards gone astray?
Have not my generals hunted down
These blaggards who betrayed my crown?

Did not our enemy retreat?
This siege obstructs supplies, depletes
Their water, barley, grain, and meat
Until they starve, and we defeat.
Tell me then, why would they run?
This deed my grace and honor shuns!
No battle had they left to fight,
Just sit and wait, both day and night;
Swill ale and feast till comes the day
The enemy yields, their lords we flay,
Then home they march, their whores to pay!"

'Twere a moment 'fore an answer came.
When spake the knight yet once again,
The King spied fear behind his eyes
As fear within did swift arise.

"I beseech thee, sire, to understand,
These men were loyal to your command!
They did not flee, this truth we dread ...
All legions four have vanishèd!
Not one amongst them have we found,
No sight or smell; no trace nor sound.
'Twas like a hole had opened 'round,
And all were swallowed by the ground!

Bewitched we are, the generals say,
Thus sent me forth from far away
To beg thee, let thy men return,
Pray let the witch that did this burn;
For blessings, all those cursèd yearn!"

Scoffing at the feckless plea
The King, by order, thus decreed:
"Steadfast, men must stay and fight!"
Aflame with anger, fiery spite,
He raised on high his blade with might;
Spilled entrails of the hapless knight!

Enraged, he kicked the chamber door;
Eavesdropping, there the Prince he saw.
So dragging his son by locks of his hair
T'ward the throne, with hateful glare,
Said, "Never will this be thy chair!
This vow 'pon mother's life I swear!
At birth, I should have put thee down,
Submerged thy face and watched thee drown!
Too weak and pale to wear my crown,
Wield swords, adorned in maiden's gowns!
Missing are 400 men,
And would I get them back again
By carving thee from ear to ear,
I'd do so with my conscience clear!"

Turning then to walk away,
He heard not what the boy did say:
"What thou didst vow upon this day,
Be wary of the game I play!"

When the morning cockerel awakened all,
The King unto his wife did call,
Yet nowhere could the Queen be found
In the castle, pantry, keep or grounds.

Though maids in waiting scoured the halls,
Her whereabouts none could recall;
Then from the fields where oft she'd dwell,
There came a sudden, piercing yell!

For in the meadow, by a brook,
The hounds found buried half a foot,
Then digging deeper, the Queen they found
Face-first planted in the ground.
Lifeless, ankle-deep and bound.

Screamed the King as they exhumed
The Queen from 'neath her earthen tomb:
"So swear I, by God, my Lord,
Vengeance shall my bloody sword
Take 'pon the wretch who did this deed!
Pain he'll feel! Slow death to bleed!
For carried he my love away
And buried her alive this day;
No quarter shall I give when slay,
And disembowel this wicked prey!"

The priest then spake, "Be calm, my son;
The mystery here has yet begun.
Inside her fingernails fresh blood,
Torn and chipped; caked with mud,
Suggests the culprit was no knave.
With her own hands dug she her grave,
Then face-first in the ditch she slid.
I'd wager 'twas a crone who did
Bewitch our Queen and got her rid;
Used black arts, holy laws forbid.

But odd as all of that might be,
One detail sits not well with me ...

For something there beneath the ground,
Was dug up by the royal hounds:
A wooden piece from the game of chess,
'Tis truth, this sleuth now stands here vexed.
Coincidence? It might well be,
Yet strange it is, wouldst thou agree?
For 'twere no bishop, knight, or rook,
No king, nor pawn placed by her foot.
The piece the hounds found in the mound
Was a queen, stuck head-first, upside down,
Same way as was Her Highness found!"

Wider grew the eyes of the King,
And said he not another thing.
As chills spilled down his spine, his gasp
Was heard by all, none dared to ask
If shadowed guilt within him lay,
But all at court could see that day
'Twas something more the King construed;
Dark secret kept, another knew.

    Then to the castle, fast he flew,
    The Queen's assassin to subdue!

Within the tower's lockèd room,
A token once found in a tomb:
A chessboard, brought forth from the grave
Of an ancient, dark and cunning mage.
This to the King great power gave,
And triumph in all wars he waged.
By moving pieces in the game,
All enemies he overcame
With checkmate, as he trapped the king,
Victory this move would bring.
Yet pieces, cursed, when moved amiss
By any other hands than his,
Caused bad luck struck, for ruin came
When any other touched his game.

And there atop the stairs he found
The door unlocked, and none around.
Thus, entering the room with care,
Cast t'ward the board his solemn stare.
Each pawn, a legion; gone were four,
Like those that vanished from the war.
And also missing was the queen,
Her death, the work of hands unseen;
'Twas a foul, atrocious, odious scheme!

He stood aghast when at last he saw
Three pieces gone, perchance yet more:
A wooden bishop, rook, and king,
Revealed did wield hate's loathsome sting;
The pendulum of guilt doth swing
T'ward son whose deeds misfortune brings!

So summoned the King his priest, and then
They searched the grounds till evening when
They spied the boy atop a tree,
Mocking those beneath him be.

The King said, "Son, pray, did you thieve
My key, wherefore? I searched this eve
Inside a room known to me just,
Where prying eyes betraying trust
Are gouged from skulls with dagger's thrust,
Then rolling o'er the floor are crushed!
And from the chessboard, did you steal
The pieces, tucked in fleece, concealed
Until such time, thought best, ideal;
Their magic to my Queen reveal?"

This waif of lad looked down below
At one, who rather than bestow
His title, would first see him dead
Than place a crown upon his head, said:

"At swordplay, bad though I may be,
A mind have I, and eyes to see.
For years that secret room I spied,
At evensong, you'd sneak inside.
When fast asleep and drunk on wine,
In waiting, I did bide my time,
Then entering, I saw laid bare
The fabled chessboard, cursed and rare.

Whoever did your men surround
'Pon battlefield, in time, I found
The same was mirrored on the board
Each time a victory was scored.

With strategy, you move your men,
Like pawns upon the chessboard, then
With rooks and knights, so wins the war,
And in this way you know for sure
Come checkmate swift or drawn by stealth,
Thou canst but win against thyself!

This magic game meant more to thee
Than I, thy boy, could ever be.
So sitting on the throne last night,
With oath, fates sown, I took delight:
    'Never will this be thy chair.
      This vow 'pon mother's life I swear!'
These reckless words did curse the Queen;
Once tempted, ill fate intervened.

My sister chosen as thine heir,
I ripped apart from loins to hair.
Now one remains, that one I be,
The future King, by law's decree!

Thus with these deeds the crown I claim,
But what then of this oath thought tame?
On mother's life so callously
You swore a vow, I crept to see
The magic board, and stole the queen;
Awoken from her sleep serene,
Mother followed I, her son,
Till the light of dawn upon us shone,
Then I placed the chess piece 'neath the ground
Same way as was my mother found.
Just like the pawns I stole last week,
You'll find them if it's truth you seek ...
Your men lie drowned beneath a creek!

400 at the bottom float,
When pawns were cast into the moat.
Behold, I hold three pieces, see?
And now the bishop I'll set free
After counting ... 1 ... 2 ... 3!"

Then as the chess piece hit the ground,
There came a most horrific sound.
By hands unseen, the priest rose up
High 'bove the tree, and like the bishop,
Crashed below and cracked his bones
Till last breath drawn 'twixt painful groans.
Smiled wide, the boy with a heart of stone;
His mouth agape, King stood alone.

He begged, "Attend thy father's plea!
Harken! Climb down from the tree,
For the error of my ways I see,
Amends I wish to make with thee!
My boy, thou art my flesh and blood,
Reviled, thought vile, deprived of love,
Yet now I see how ruthlessly
My son hath proved his worth to me.
For callous hearts all mercy lack
As thwart their foes in fierce attack.
This brutal lesson, finally learned,
Respect from me is justly earned.

With a magic board and the game of chess,
Aligned, shall we our foes repress,
Both cruel and fierce and merciless,
With none to challenge our success,
For none have powers we possess!"

But the little Prince, he listened not,
For love, alas, his heart forgot.
So took he the rook and took he the king
And close by one did the other bring,
Then using spellcraft, cold and planned,
Crushed both together in his hand.

What happened next, none can explain,
Yet some say signs there still remain
This very day, if ye look, will find
The ruined castle left behind.
If legends told can be believed,
This picture with ye I shall leave:

A castle rising up from the ground,
Each brick, each wall, and turret round
Hanging there, was hurled toward
The scheming, screaming King, abhorred,
By a magical force, so the tale doth record.

Crushed was the King, his son the same;
With both died sigil, family name,
Then brush and brambles overcame,
The land's lush forest rose again,
Till none remembered those once slain.

Still, some do think the legends true,
And in the woods they dig anew,
Hoping there that find they might
A pawn or bishop, king, or knight,
Or a magic board this long survived,
Its power might they then revive,
And play at chess to conquer all;
To make, at will, great kingdoms fall,
Just like the King who love did lack,
O'er daughter fawned, spawned son's attack.
Repaid was he for scorn and hate,
Sent down below where darkness waits.
Sold short his foe; 'twas grave mistake,
For vengeance, boy did undertake
A perfect plan, cooked slow then baked,
With rook to king
... Said he, "checkmate."

Yet pieces, cursed, when moved amiss by any other hands than his
caused bad luck struck, for ruin came
when any other touched his game.

Script for a Jester's Tear

England, 1211.

Author's Note: I had first heard about a creature called a *Jŏstas* in school during a history project on Sutton Hoo, the Anglo-Saxon burial site unearthed in Suffolk, England, in 1939. Among the artifacts uncovered there, we were told that some bore markings of a mysterious phrase, one that appeared frequently in manuscripts and stone carvings from 410 AD to around 1000 AD. *Waria þā Jŏstases tēaras,* literally translated, means *Beware the tears of the Jŏstas.* Just who (or what) a *Jŏstas* might be is anyone's guess. Some dismissed it as a misreading of a funerary blessing; others believed it to be part of a now-lost oral tradition, possibly connected to pagan ritual, early Christian demonology, or a long-forgotten folkloric warning. Sadly, any writings that could have shed light on its true origins have either been lost to time or remain undiscovered. What is known is this: whether viewed through the lens of academic history or conspiracy theory, the *Jŏstas*—be it man or beast—is universally considered malevolent. Its tears, as the phrase suggests, are not merely sorrowful but dangerous. Thanks in no small part to that timely school project at an impressionable age, I became fixated on the shrieking, weeping creature of legend. *What was a Jŏstas? Why does it cry?* And most importantly, *why were the hardened Anglo-Saxons scared when it did?*

Thankfully, that haunting curiosity didn't follow me into adulthood. In fact, I had forgotten about *Jŏstas* completely until recently, when I stumbled across a strange and mildly unsettling tale from the collection of Simon de Montfort, the 6th Earl of Leicester. The story was entitled, *Giacomo* (pronounced *Jack-a-moe*). Intrigued, I looked into its origins and found it was more commonly known in medieval European courts by its alternate title: *Script for a Jester's Tear.*

Then it struck me: *Jŏstases Tēaras—Jester's Tears*. The similarity seemed too obvious to ignore. Had the Anglo-Saxons discovered something nefarious and were trying to warn us of the court's resident fool and his weeping? Or was a *Jŏstas* something far older, and darker—an evil entity born before the days of man? Or perhaps, as this chilling 13th-century tale seems to suggest, the ancient creature of malevolence and the beloved court clown were, in fact, one and the same.

'Twas on the eve of Cristes mæsse,
These fates untold yet came to pass
When unannounced at court he came,
And did before the queen proclaim
His name was Giacomo, the fool,
Then bumbling, stumbling on his shoe
He tottered with the poise and grace
Of a goat on ice, with pained face
And garments silken, bright and gaye,
As reeled in folly, jolly play
Before the queen, then on his seat,
He sprawled and smiled in mocked defeat.

The queen bemused, yet filled with cheer,
Did gesture to the jester, "here."
And beckoned forth, the fool took stand,
Hearkening to the royal command,
He stirred, then surged from lying prone,
Did somersets t'ward the throne;
Swept low, as reeds in raging winds,
Effecting such a bow, as grinned,
And to the dumbstruck queen, exclaimed,
"'Tis from a realm beyond, I came;
A gift, sent forth 'cross land and sea,
To please your royal majesty!"

The queen inquired, "What lord, or liege
Sent forth his fool whose wit lays siege
To somber clouds that shroud my court?"
Replied the fool with swift retort:
"'Twas he whose seal this message bears.
A loyal servant, one who shares,
And cares, and loves, and lives to serve.
Make merry; feast thy souls on mirth,
For I here I stand, in all the land,
None such as I exist, for bland
Seem other clowns, when so compared
Are woesome, loathsome, wit-impaired.
Bring forth what fool that here doth dwell.
He'll bow to thee and me as well!"

"No fool have we," the queen declared,
"For jesting is a talent rare
That few possess, or mayhap less;
We are, then, by thy presence blessed.
Impertinent, and hubris-filled,
As you may be, 'tis want fulfilled
Thanks be these noble tidings sent.
Let cheer be known, let tears relent!"

The jester, with a furrowed brow
Said, "Majesty, pray tell me how
This veil of sorrow came to be
That smothers all, save only me?"

The queen, her head hung low, took pause,
Then unto him divulged the cause:
"My king doth languish in his health,
And no elixirs, jewels, or wealth,
Nor potions brewed by cackling crones
Can ease his ailing, aching bones.

Mayhap then, might the answer be
A jester: fester's remedy?
For if your japes give rise to laughter,
My realm lives happ'ly ever after!"

And so, the jester went to where
The bishop knelt in solemn prayer
Beside the bed where lay the king,
A pallid shade of gray and green.
And though the jester pranced and fell,
And danced with tricks and quips he'd tell,
Cavorting, courting smiles and glee,
None did come, and all could see
The king, forspent, was fading fast.
The queen, perturbed, the fool then asked:
"The king of clowns the land throughout?
Of talents, men from rooftops shout?
Such was your claim, you did exclaim,
Yet scarce a smile nor flicker came
To stir the king's dry purple lips,
Despite your riddles, tricks and quips.
So how, straight faced, can you profess
Such skills possessed to jest impress?"

Hearing thus the queen's rebuke,
Giacomo then quoth the duke
Whose letter, sealed with noble crest,
Sent forth the jester as bequest,
And begged her read what there was writ,
For more than waggery and wit,
The fool did hide a hidden gift,
Avowing spirits felled shall lift!

"Yet such a gift comes with a catch,
So wrote the one who did dispatch,
That Giacomo will not reveal,"
Said she, as split the wax on seal
And read aloud the message scribed
Upon the scroll, eyes growing wide.
"For 'tis," quoth she, "the task of we
To find what hidden faculty
This vexing clown here doth possess,
For he can tell us not, nor bless
Any, till his skill's discovered."
Glowering then upon the mummer,
Said the queen, "What is thy use?
This secret now we must deduce?

Thy tongue is tied to speak with truth,
Thy humor failed, here lies the proof!
What talents veiled do you possess
To lift the king from his distress?
This duke bestowed thee unto me,
Yet revels in the comedy
That here thou art, his 'master clown,'
With a secret unrevealed till found!
No further use have I for thee.
Return from whence you came, what sea
What land was crossed, cross back once more
To where your smirk did lurk before!"

Crimson turned the jester's face,
As languid, swallowed by disgrace,
He paced about the place and fell
Upon his knees; his eyes did well,
And lo, upon his cheek, appeared
The trail of but a single tear ...

And seeing this, the queen was shook,
'Pon weeping fool, her pity took,
And kneeling by him, gently placed
A palm of comfort on his face;
Caressed his cheek and softly spoke
To quell the fire her ire had stoked.

For never must a jester cry,
And if they do, ten children die,
Four score of angels downward fall
From Heaven's realm, rough seas and squalls
Shake sailors' ships, and thus thou art
From that day forth, by mischance marked!

'Twas then a miracle occurred ...
For as the queen, her pity stirred,
Gently stroked the jester's face,
A transformation then took place.
As she dried his tears down cheek and chin
The hue of youth reclaimed her skin.
Her knuckles supple, tight, not dry,
As a virgin maiden's milky thighs.
All spots and creases disappeared,
Each wart and wrinkle, crinkle cleared!

"The secret lies thy tears within!"
The queen proclaimed to court and kin,
"Sweet Giacomo, pray weep once more!
Your tears my luster must restore!
From heaven's heights this fool did fall,
I urge thee blubber, wail and bawl!
Your precious water, priceless pearls
Of blessed liquid, dukes and earls
And barons gather, see, behold,
What wondrous gift this jester holds!"

Then to the queen there did arise
A notion born of keen surmise,
That if a jester's tear reversed
All signs of age, could they disperse
What malady beset her king?
And if such drops about would bring
His restoration from disease,
Few droplets of this liquid eased
From 'twixt the eyes, when next he cries,
Might king and queen cheat fate, ne'er die?

And with these tears the king was cured,
With fortunes of their realm secured,
As king and queen in tears did bathe,
By decades each reversed their age.
And Giacomo did entertain.
Laughter did resound again
Around the court where once a pin,
If dropped, would cause a mighty din,
Until the eve the king did call
Upon the jolly jester, sprawled
Across the floor, before his throne,
With grin, mid-spin, ere lying prone.

"Giacomo, my lord buffoon,
Sweet jack-a-napes, my motley goon,
A favor of thee I must ask:
Take to thy chamber, fill my flask
Up to the brim with tears of sorrow,
Joy, or pain, then on the morrow,
Bring unto me this that you've cried,
So I may bathe my royal bride
And soak away the lines of time,
Reverse the years; hers first, then mine."

But Giacomo could weep no more,
For rare is such, so sayeth lore
And legends, thus a jester's tears
Are jewels of great renown revered.

At this, the king became enraged,
And locked the fool inside a cage,
Within the dungeon, then the rack
Tore sinews, stretched, near broke his back.
Yet thumbscrews, red hot pokers, all,
Caused not a single tear to fall.
For torturing can only fail;
It bears no fruit, provokes no wails.
"This pain," the king with ire proclaimed,
"Is not the way to win this game!"

Then cats and hounds he did parade
Outside the jester's squalid cage.
As cat-o'-nine tails tore their skin,
Their howls did stir the fool within
To beg him stop, and thus compelled,
From red, wet eyes, two rivers fell.

This spite the king and queen did show
Did not without comeuppance go.
For fate dealt sorrows crushing blow,
Returning thrice in kind their woe ...

A bucket full of jester's tears
Had they to wash away their years,
But as their spots and wrinkles faded,
So too their minds, keen wits and age did.
Children, thus, they both became,
Nigh three feet tall in height, and frame
That of a bairn, whelp, babe, or brat;
Upon their thrones, engulfed, they sat.
And with this, Giacomo the fool
Revealed to them true colors cruel ...

The note he pressed the king to yield,
With wax, by royal signet sealed,
Revealed the jester was a gift
That sullen spirits, sunk, would lift.
And this he'd take where next he roamed,
As was the ruse the jester honed,
Picking victims from the herd
Of lords and kings he'd feigned to serve.

Then in the sight of royal babes,
Cavorted then contorted, blades
Where once were teeth appeared to sprout,
As through his face there tore a snout.
About him, like a shed cocoon,
Molted skin and flesh lay strewn,
As moths discard their larval tomb,
Revealing thus, this bane of doom.

Where stood a man, now slithered beast.
'Pon toddler fodder fangs did feast,
As first the queen he swallowed whole;
His mouth once, now a gaping hole,
Consumed the wretched king that ruled
The kingdom, wanton, crass and cruel,
With lust for long gone years of yore,
Was by this creature torn in four.

Epilogue:
What e'er it was, none here could say,
For since time's dawn on man it preyed,
This entity as old as time,
Walks unpunished for its crimes
Hunting that 'pon which it feasts,
Sustained by children's flesh, this beast
Assumes a fool's beloved guise
To infiltrate and stalk its prize:
Nobles, blood of royal blue,
Their tender veins it doth pursue.
Tears make them young, then as years drop,
They're chewed to mangled, bloodied slop.

Thus, should a fool, his fame pronounced,
Appear at court e'er, unannounced,
Pray, keep him happy. Make him smile.
Unto thy years be reconciled.
For should this jester shed a tear,

'Tis more than age ye have to fear ...

Tears make them young, then as years drop,
They're chewed to mangled, bloodied slop.

The William Tree

13th century. The village of Gayhurst, Buckinghamshire, England.
Said by locals to be a true story. I pray to God they are wrong.

In the middle of a field there stood
A sacred tree of oaken wood,
Planted, so the elders say,
By a Norman King who came that way.

A bloody battle had he won,
Thus, in this field, King William,
To mark the ground none dared despoil,
With his own hands, put seed to soil,
To grow, and so remember all
This victory had made to fall.

With prayer, declared there holy ground;
Forbade all men for miles around,
To enter the field where stood the tree,
Or the wrath of God upon them be.

Two hundred years hence from that day,
None go near and shy away;
All damned who do, the Abbots say,
Thus, towns still fear, adhere, obey.

The son of a local Duke was he,
Oft gazed upon it wistfully,
And dream, for had he in his mind,
One summer's day, this tree he'd climb.
But father warned as father 'fore,
"Take not a step thee closer more.
That tree hath yet its curse concealed,
Till oath be spurned, its bane is sealed."

One day to the village graveyard dared,
With sister, to provoke a scare
And tumbled down into a cave,
Where crumbled bones and flesh decayed
'Neath roots of trees; the stench of graves
Effused throughout the cold enclaves.

Back on their feet, more shook than hurt,
Declared the boy, "Be brave, alert.
A secret tunnel we have found,
From all eyes hidden 'neath the ground.
See how all the coffins here
Lie open, bodies gone? 'Tis queer.
If we descend this shaft below,
More secrets then we'd surely know.
Recovering bodies is our task;
What knave disturbs death's sleep, unmask!

Sister, be thou not afraid;
Stay close and trust thy brother brave.
Dost thou see not every grave
Has been defiled a similar way?
The smallest coffins are the ones
Of babies, children, daughters, sons,
Their lids removed and bodies gone;
We've much to prove, let's venture on!"

So through the tunnel in the dark,
To solve this riddle, not for lark,
They crawled for half a mile until
Ahead, they saw the sunlight spill.
Closer now than lore abides,
Than any other souls alive,
Alone within the field they spied
Branches lush and sprawling wide.

"Reached have we the tunnel's end
That from the field to graveyard sends
Any with a size this small,"
Said boy, "and bold as we who crawl."

'Twas then that something caught their eyes,
Before them, on the tree they spied
The bark that shimmered in the sun,
A golden brown, had now become
Clear, no more a distant blur,
But something else ... with legs ... and fur.

Too scared to speak, both realized
Ten thousand legs with fangs and eyes,
And larger size, near half a cat,
Or quarter dog; some twice a rat,
From branches' tip to roots below,
At distance none would ever know,
But lo, close as they'd come to be,
Spied spiders swarming up the tree!

Both whispered, begged for God to bless,
Lest breaths disturb this giant nest.
With a finger placed on her brother's lips,
Said sister, "Silence! Let us slip
Back through the tunnel ... go! Make haste!
'Fore sweet our flesh the spiders taste!"

Deep in the tunnel, gripped by fear,
A wrong turn taken drew them near
To where the cursèd tree took root;
There what they saw made siblings mute:
Bodies taken from the graves,
In webs 'twixt eggs the spiders laid;
From rotting flesh, their brood then hatched,
So back they pressed, lest they be snatched.

And there behind, they saw red eyes;
Black fangs as sharp as Reaper's scythes,
So through the cavern, fast away
As legs would carry, prayers both prayed,
Then brother tripped; head struck the floor;
Remembered he then nothing more.

Awoken gently in his bed,
By fire, with pillow 'neath his head,
Safe and warm inside his home,
Far from the cave where spiders roam.
There by his side, the Abbot sighed,
A shaken head, his grief implied.

Said holy man, "You must be shook,
For a grievous fright this night you took."
Asked boy, "My sister, harm befell?"
Said Abbot, "Hush, and hear me well.

Both you and sister disobeyed;
To the sacred field took ye to play,
And there beheld on the William Tree
What none are ever meant to see.

King William, who conquered all,
For men who did in battle fall,
Planted there the tree, and lo,
'Tis sacred ground where none may go.
But spirits, they of the men who fell,
Though lives be lost, so legends tell,
Refused to turn the other cheek;
'Pon towns around did vengeance seek.
For townsfolk, by gold's lure deceived,
With Norman Lords, a pact conceived:
A plot to turn the battle's tide,
And make the foe their friend, allied.

Outnumbered then, the battle lost,
The dead swore all would pay the cost.
They bargained with the spiders dread
For traitors' kin to eat when dead.
Five towns surround that field, you see,
Whose men conspired with treachery,
Thus, did the tree's foul curse begin
And eight-legged beasts do nest therein.

They feast on rotting babes in graves;
If left to this, all lives are saved,
But now disturbed, the swarm enraged,
Fresh flesh ensures their wrath's assuaged.

Thy sister was our sacrifice;
Her meat for thy misdeeds, the price.
And so appeased, they're held at bay ...
But what of thee who slipp'd away?

Canst thou see both hands are tied?
Now harken well, I shall confide.
A boil you have upon thy wrist
Will fill with pus, and from this cyst,
A baby spider out will pop,
And cause thy flesh beneath to rot.

For in the tunnel when you fell,
Its mother placed her egg there well
And let you live, its host to be;
Once born, eight legs shall scurry free."

The boy glanced at his wrists bound tight;
Beheld his father's troubled plight
With mother, crying, both as prayed
For a wayward son who disobeyed,
And a daughter's soul death stole that day.

Said the boy, "What fate shall be
For seeing that which I saw on the tree?
If losing an arm shall pay the price,
Though painful be my sacrifice,
We may yet warn all folk herein
And burn what horror dwells within!"

The Abbot said, "'Tis not the plan,"
Dismissing parents with his hand.
Then locking the door, up close he came
And whispered, "Worse you'll be than lame."
As he lifted the sheets so the lad could see
On chest, one hundred boils had he;
On stomach more, down legs and feet,
The hatchling spiders soon would eat.

Inside lad's mouth, he stuffed a rag,
For screams of agony to gag.
Then said, "Steadfast against the horde,
Our forebears fought with a mace and sword
Bravely for this English land,
But crushed were they by William's hand
Thanks be to traitors in these towns
Whose foul plot cut their fellows down.

Their spirits were the ones who did
Cede the tree to arachnids,
Thus, William's final legacy
Forever is accursed, we
Shall veil the tale, for when you die,
So does the truth that with thee lies.

As spiders feast on flesh of babes,
Our lives go on familiar ways.
A treat you'll be, for still alive,
Sweet be your meat; their young shall thrive.
Feed them full and fare thee well;
'Tis the only way, lest thou should tell
The secret of the William Tree,
So all may live, must die with thee."

Then on his wrist the blister popped;
Fang's hungry kiss could not be stopped ...

Jacobite Lights

Late 17th century, Scotland. From a private collection belonging to
William Johnstone, 1st Marquess of Annandale.

In British history, a Jacobite was the name given to those loyal to the
exiled King James II, supporting the restoration of the House of Stuart to
the British throne. James, a Catholic, had been deposed in the "Glorious
Revolution" and replaced by his Protestant sister Mary II and her husband,
William of Orange. This provoked outrage among Catholics and Stuart
supporters who believed only God could appoint a monarch, not Parliament.
By May 1690, Jacobite uprisings fought primarily in Scotland had largely
been suppressed, with the Scottish government agreeing to pay the Jacobite
clans a total of £12,000 in return for an oath of loyalty to William and
Mary; however, disagreements among the chiefs over its division meant that
by the following year, they still had not sworn the oath. Several months
later, the infamous Massacre of Glencoe took place, whereby Scottish
government forces killed an estimated 30 members of Clan MacDonald of
Glencoe for failing to pledge allegiance to the new monarchs. Persecution of
Jacobites throughout Scotland escalated.

The deposed king's grandfather, the House of Stuart's founding father,
King James VI of Scotland (later also James I of England), had written a
book called *Dæmonology* several years before the first publication of the
King James authorized version of the Bible. *Dæmonology* discussed the
devil's persecution of men and endorsed the practice of witch-hunting. An
estimated 4,000 suspected witches were tortured and burned in Scotland
following its publication.

With the exception of a few archaic colloquialisms and slang (decipherable in the glossary), these are the facts you must know to follow this terrible tale, based on actual events, that took place on a stormy All Hallows Eve in 1692. Although not medieval, I have included Jacobite Lights for two reasons. Firstly, this version was sourced from the book *Angst bei die Schlafenszeit* (Anxiety at Bedtime), an infamous collection of horrible short stories used to punish misbehaving children of Prussian nobility. Secondly, and in my opinion most importantly, is its historical significance to my favorite holiday, Halloween. If the tale is indeed true, as many claim it to be, it explains why carving pumpkins became a "thing." Although after reading it, you may never feel quite the same way about doing that "thing" again.

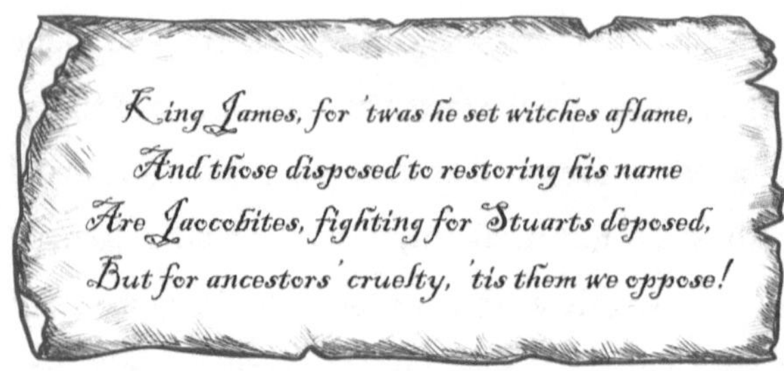

Outside the gates of the convent they came,
The torn, careworn strangers, nae smock, boots, or name,
Nor shame, as they pounded wet fists on the door
Set on waking the dead, seven nuns, though, before,
Three staggering blaggards, all ravaged by war.

Begging the sisters for water and food,
Shelter from weather and a fierce bloody feud.
"Slaughtered like dogs, us true men of the creed
Loyal to King James and the Pope," they did plead.
"Clan MacDonald of Glencoe, thirty or more,
Cut down for the king, papists say evermore
Was anointed by God, nae that blasphemous whore!"

Said their one, "Here we've come, for the battle we've lost.
Refusing to pledge our allegiance has cost
Brave Jacobite lives, those shunning the oath
Swearing fealty to Mary and William both;
Cross the country from Glencoe, we fled to Arbroath.

And sharing with thee, as do we, blessed faith,
I trust three of us with you here will be safe
From the Protestant zealots, foul dæmons disguised!
'Tis three heads they'll take of the kind they despise.
For they banished the king; now they seek our demise!"

'Neath the feet of the sisters, they groveled and wept,
Pleading for bread, for divine faith be kept
By each as they fought for the Catholic cause.
Surely merciful nuns should consent without pause?
Wind blustered; strength mustered; they pushed through the doors!

The nuns gathered, fearful of three who'd intruded,
For no news of war reached the convent secluded.
As was asked, so they passed bread and water to all;
Came the Mother Superior, stirred by the call
Of the three who sought rest from a fierce highland squall.

"'Tis for James that was exiled to France that you fight.
Men as thee, sworn to be, call yourselves Jacobites.
For a protestant queen now sits on the throne,"
Said the Mother, "Her faith, none in here will condone.
But James' father, Charles, and the father of he
Was the sixth James of Scotland, says the family tree,
Or the first James of England when united became.
Son of Mary of Scots, once beheaded, the same;
The royal house of Stuart, their family name."

Then one of the nuns passing water and bread
Dropped her basket and jug, hearing words Mother said.
As a thunderous roar from the clouds filled the room
Echoed moans 'twixt the stones of the dark convent tomb.
Lightning lit Mother's face o'er the men as she loomed.

Said the Mother Superior, "This house that ye serve,
The Stuarts, whose words blessed faith did preserve
When James wrote a book, the sixth of his name;
A treatise of ways that a witch might be tamed.
Those who practiced the craft for misfortune he blamed,
Encouraging all to put flesh to the flame.

At the witch trials of Berwick, one hundred were took
And tortured because of the words in this book.
Thousands they captured and thousands they burned
Awaiting Christ's rapture, same men to beasts turned,
Killing innocent souls, sacred martyrdom earned
By facing the fire, were by heaven nae spurned.

But a few witches true also suffered that fate,
Whose master's black seed in their souls did gestate,
Tied to a pole and roasted alive,
By men of the faith that colluded, connived
... Yet tales that we heard say a few still survived."

"'Twas James in his book said we should persecute
Those who practice the craft; in its ways resolute,"
Said one Jacobite, "Now their kind's few to none,
Thanks be King James, but the crown from the son
Of his son has been taken; this kingdom is done!

Blessed communion is our humble request.
Seeking favor, we'll labor; toil at your behest.
Far we have traveled, for months day and night,
Now assume to commune with ye here if we might?
Be not leery of road-weary three Jacobites."

Then the wind whipped and whistled throughout the dark halls
Outing the flames of the torches; them all.
And there, in the darkness, the nuns all joined hands,
Voices raised in a chant to the Jacobite clan;
Surrounding them, sisters hissed whispered commands.

"Behold, the storm rages out there in the night,
And the fierce, gusting, thrusting wind outed our lights.
Many months have you traveled, opponents deceived,
And arrived have you here 'pon this dark Hallows Eve,
... But none here are nuns ... this you've falsely perceived.

This convent's a coven and witches we are,
Persecuted as are thee, you three traveled far!
'Twas the bloodline of Stuart that drove our kind down
Concealed by the shadows, we hide from the towns
Disguised in these wimples and white holy gowns.

Ye Jacobites all might one day get your way
When your Catholic king wears the crown, then someday,
The deplored house of Stuart will set us aflame,
So we spit on their cross and profane their cruel name,
And those in their service we consider fair game!"

Entranced, as did sisters their vile witches' dance,
Seduced by bare bosoms, bewitched by their chants,
Three Jacobites yielded and spilled did their seed
Betwixt the nuns' cunnies their pintles made bleed
Till the devil's vile brides had the fill that they need.

With their ritual done, dark duties fulfilled,
And each witch's loin filled with sauce Jacobites spilled,
Said unto the others, the queen of the coven:
"Now bake we fresh buns in each of our ovens,
Our hallways are dark, our torches are dead,
Come, let us separate each of their heads,
Strip them bare to the skull to make lanterns instead!"

And there, as a storm raged on All Hallows Eve,
Three Jacobites, witches had made to spill seed,
God's mercy or pardon none there did receive
No amnesty, respite, delay, or reprieve,
As with saws, knives, and blades, witches finished their deed.

The passage that follows, years later, was found
When both convent and coven were burned to the ground:

King James, for 'twas he set witches aflame,
And those disposed to restoring his name
Are Jacobites, fighting for Stuarts deposed,
But for ancestors' cruelty, 'tis them we oppose!
We carved their heads hollow; placed a candle inside
Made with wax from their gut fat, burns longer and bright.
Through eye holes and gaping jaws spilled forth the flame
And a Jacobite Lantern, each then became.
"This name is a mouthful. Let's cut it short,"
Said I, "Jacko-Lanterns, to call them, we ought!"

To those loyal to the Devil this kingdom throughout,
Do as we did to those Stuarts devout!
But if one can't be found to spill seed in your bed
And no light can ye carve from a Jacobite's head,
In remembrance of how we bewitched them that night,
When an All Hallows wind blew and outed our lights,
Make hollow a gourd, and a candle there place,
For a pumpkin on Halloween night can replace
A bright Jaco-Lantern, smile carved on its face

...So sayeth we witches refuting God's grace!

Through eye holes and gaping jaw spilled forth the flame
and a Jacobite Lantern, each then became.
"This name is a mouthful. Let's cut it short,"
said I, "Jacko-Lanterns, to call them, we ought!"

Glossary

Old words are hard. Let's end your suffering right here, right now.

Afore- Before.

Alchemist- Practitioner of Alchemy.

Alchemy- A medieval chemical science and speculative philosophy aiming to achieve the transmutation of the base metals into gold, the discovery of a universal cure for disease, and the discovery of a means of indefinitely prolonging life.

Ale- An alcoholic beverage darker and heavier than beer, as in Newcastle Brown Ale, which exists today. Try it, you'll like it.

Bairn- Young child or baby. The word is chiefly used in Scotland and northern England, and it has Old English and Norse roots.

Bard- A poet, traditionally one reciting or singing epics and associated with a particular oral tradition.

Baron/ Baroness- A Nobleman/ Noblewoman and member of the aristocracy.

Battlements- A parapet at the top of a castle wall that has regularly spaced squared openings for shooting through.

Beseech- Implore.

Betwixt (also 'twixt)- Between.

Black Magic (Magic Dark)- A type of magic that conjures and communicates with malevolent spirits to do harmful things.

Blaggard- A colloquial or informal way of pronouncing and spelling the word "blackguard." It refers to a scoundrel, an unprincipled or contemptible person.

Boar- A tusked, wild pig.

Canst- Can.

Cat-o'-nine tails- A multi-tailed whip.

Chateau- French, meaning "castle."

Clocked- Slang term for "hit" or "struck."

Codpiece- a covering flap or pouch that attaches to the front of the crotch of men's trousers, enclosing the genital area.

Cowl- An item of clothing consisting of a long, hooded garment with wide sleeves.

Cristes mæsse- Old English term for Christmas.

Crone- In folklore, a crone was a malicious old woman with supernatural or magical associations.

Cunny- Crass, Middle-English slang for female genitalia.

Cursèd- Pronounced cur-sed.

Davy Jones- Lead singer of The Monkees, but not in this case. Davy Jones's locker is a metaphor for the bottom of the sea: It is sometimes used as a euphemism for drowning.

Dist- Did. (Duh!)

Dost- Archaic second person singular present of "do."

Doth- Archaic third person singular present of "do."

Dowry- Property or money brought by a bride to her husband on their marriage.

Duchess/Duke- Duchess is a female title and Duke is a male title of a monarch ruling over a duchy, or of a member of royalty, or nobility. As rulers, dukes are ranked below emperors, kings, grand princes, grand dukes, and sovereign princes.

Duchy- A dominion or region ruled by a duke or duchess.

Dwarven - Of, pertaining to or made by or for dwarfs/dwarves.

Dæmon- Archaic spelling of the word "demon," meaning an evil spirit thought to possess a person or act as a tormentor in hell.

Entreat- Implore.

Ere- Before. Not to be confused with "e'er" which is a contraction of "ever." Confused?

Evensong/E'ensong- Evening.

Fealty- Formal acknowledgment of loyalty to a lord, i.e., "they owed fealty to the King."

Ferryman- According to Greek mythology, to be properly buried, a coin called an obol needed to be placed under your tongue. This would then be presented to Charon- the Ferryman of the Styx (the river, not the band), as payment for crossing the river to the underworld.

Flagon- A large container in which a drink is served, typically with a handle and spout.

Forsooth- Indeed.

Friar- A friar belongs to a religious order, a group within the Catholic church, especially the four mendicant orders: Augustinians, Carmelites, Dominicans, and Franciscans, devoted to religious life. Unlike a monk, a Friar lives and works among regular people in society, while a monk lives in a secluded group.

Gnome- European folklore. A dwarfish, subterranean goblin, or earth spirit who guards mines of precious treasures hidden in the earth.

Grog- Liquor (such as rum) cut with water.

Habit- A long, loose garment worn by a member of a religious order or congregation.

Hades- The underworld. Hell.

Hadst- Archaic second person singular of "have."

Hands- A unit of measurement (4 inches).

Hath- Archaic third person singular present of "have."

Headsman- Executioner.

Hence- For this reason or, in the future if used after a period of time, e.g., "two years hence."

Henceforth- From this time forward.

Hi- to move quickly (hurry).

Highborn- Of noble birth. Members of the aristocracy.

Jack-a-napes- A foolish or mischievous person.

Jacobite- Members of a political movement that supported the restoration of the senior line of the House of Stuart to the British throne.

Kirtle- A long gown or dress worn by women in the

Middle- Ages.

Knave- A tricky deceitful fellow of humble birth or position.

Lazy- You. See "Internet Search Engine" above.

Legion- A large military force or a very large number of something.

Liege- A feudal lord or superior to whom allegiance and service are owed.

Liripipe- A hood with a trailing point or long tail.

Longsword- European style sword with a grip primarily for two-handed use.

Lord/Lady- Nobility. Members of the aristocracy.

Lucifer- Name for the Devil in Christian theology. The Latin word *lucifer* (uncapitalized), means "the morning star", "the planet Venus", or, as an adjective, "light-bringing."

Mace- A medieval weapon, typically having a metal head and spikes.

Magistrate- A local official exercising administrative and often judicial functions.

Maiden/Maid- An unmarried virgin.

Mariner- A sailor.

Mead- A fermented beverage made of water and honey, malt, and yeast (Tastes better than it sounds. Trust).

Mermaid- A fabled marine creature with the head and upper body of a woman and the tail of a fish. See also "Siren."

Minstrel- A medieval singer or musician.

Missal- A book containing prayers, scripture, and liturgy used during Catholic Mass.

Moat- A deep ditch dug around a castle and filled with water as a preliminary line of defense.

Mummer- Traditionally, a masked or costumed performer who performs, dances, or mimes. In medieval England, mummers entertained during Yuletide or other festivals.

Nae- Scottish English or Northern English for "no" or "not."

Nay- No.

Necromancy- Communicating with the dead to foretell the future, and/or the practice of black magic.

Neophyte- A new convert, often to a subject, skill or belief.

Ne'er- Never.

Nosferatu- An archaic Romanian word, synonymous with "vampire," but way cooler sounding.

Ogre- A hideous giant of folklore that feeds on human beings. That's right, Shrek was a cannibal. Let that sink in for a minute.

Over yon- Over there.

O'er- Over.

Page (boy or girl)- Young helper of nobles.

Pike- A long thrusting spear.

Pintle- Middle-English and Scots slang for male genitalia.

Polearm- A close combat weapon in which the main fighting part of the weapon is fitted to the end of a long shaft, typically of wood, thereby extending the user's effective range and striking power.

Pommel- The nob on the hilt of a sword (fnarr fnarr).

Portcullis- A strong, heavy grating that can be lowered to block the entrance of a castle.

Portly- Having a round, stout body.

Poseidon- The violent and ill-tempered god of the sea.

Pot-shot- Drunk and disorderly.

Pottage- A thick soup or stew of vegetables and sometimes meat.

Prithee- An alteration of "I pray thee," meaning please.

Pyre- A heap of combustible material, especially one for burning a corpse as part of a funeral ceremony or a witch.

Rack- Medieval torture device designed to inflict excruciating pain by stretching the victim's body.

Saidest/Saidst- Said.

Sayeth- Say.

Scabbard- A sheath for the blade of a sword or dagger, typically made of leather or metal.

Shank- A sharp object. Anything that looks or works like a knife.

Siren- In Greek mythology, Sirens were dangerous creatures who lured nearby sailors with their enchanting music and singing voices to shipwreck on the rocky coast of their island. See also "Mermaid."

Smite- To strike forcefully or attack.

Smock- A coat-like outer garment, often worn to protect the clothes.

Squire- In the Middle Ages, a squire was the shield or armor-bearer of a knight. The use of the term evolved over time. Initially, a squire served as a knight's apprentice.

Stocks- These were used to punish people for crimes such as swearing or drunkenness. Criminals would sit or stand at a wooden frame and the local people would throw rotten food or even stones at them.

Sup- To drink.

Tap-shackled- Drunk. In his translation of Bishop Hall's *The Discovery of a New World* (c.1609), John Healey tells of a man who, "being truly tap-shackled, mistook the window for the door."

Tarry- Wait, stay, or linger.

Thou/ Thee- You.

Thrup'ney- British informal, alternative spelling of threepenny. Pronounced "thrup-nee." Alluding to something being cheap. Which, ironically, nothing in Britain is.

Thus- Therefore. To this degree or extent.

Thy/ Thine- Your.

Tope- To drink alcohol to excess (i.e., Friday).

Tourney- Tournament.

Troth- loyal or pledged faithfulness.

Turret- A small tower on top of a larger tower or at the corner of a building or wall of a castle.

T'wards- Towards.

Vampyr- (also vampyre) is an archaic spelling of "vampire." As a point of interest, John William Polidori, who boasts the first published modern vampire story, written in 1819, used this alternative spelling. *The Vampyre* is taken from the story Lord Byron told as part of a contest among Polidori, Mary Shelley, Lord Byron, and Percy Shelley. The same contest produced the famous gothic novel *Frankenstein; or, The Modern Prometheus.*

Verily- In truth, truly.

Waggery- Playful, mischievous humor and behavior.

Ward- The strongly fortified enclosure at the heart of a medieval castle.

Wench- A young woman or girl.

Whelp- A young person, often used dismissively to imply inexperience, arrogance, or insolence.

Whence- From where or from which place.

Wraith- Spirit or undead creature. Remember the Ring Wraiths in Lord of the Rings? No? You're dead to me.

Ye- You (when referring to more than one person) or archaic spelling of "the."

Yon/Yonder- There, as in "over yonder."

'Fore- Before.

'Mongst- Amongst.

'Pon- Upon.

'Twas/ 'Twere - It was/ It were.

'Tween/'Twixt- Between.

'Twill- It will.

Every "write your own author's bio" article I have read suggests writing in the third person (which I ignored because it's silly) and to mention the credentials, professional or otherwise, qualifying me to write on the subjects presented in this book.

I have none.

I write my twisted tales of medieval macabre from my home in Nashville, Tennessee, which I share with my wife Karolina, my dog/Patronus, Alfie, my cat/dragon Balerion the Dread, and my adopted cat, Pippin. They are works of fiction dealing with, among other things, evil, maleficence, witchcraft, and the black arts, all of which I have guarded respect for but neither practice, endorse, or recommend to my readers.

I had two teachers at school who perhaps had a hand in these shenanigans. Mrs. Edwards made it fun to learn English Literature and because of her, I am a fan of Chaucer and Shakespeare. Mrs. Wright taught R.E. and encouraged me to use "my talent," as though it were some malevolent power. Maybe it is. I'm a Scorpio, an avid vinyl record collector (particularly metal and jazz), play guitar (once professionally), and love animals probably more than most humans.

My last name, von Richthofen Lyngstad, is a bit of a mouthful. Sadly, to the best of my knowledge, I am not related to the Red Baron, Manfred von Richthofen, or ABBA's Anni-Frid Lyngstad. If I were, I'd be a lot richer. And definitely prettier.